ON A WILD DUKE CHASE

COPYRIGHT

On a Wild Duke Chase
The Wayward Woodvilles, Book 2
Copyright © 2022 by Tamara Gill
Cover Art by Wicked Smart Designs
Editor Grace Bradley Editing, LLC

ISBN: 978-0-6454177-6-0

CHAPTER
ONE

Woodville House, 1805

Isla Woodville threw rose petals at her sister Hailey, now the Duchess of Derby, as she ran through the line of family and friends with her new husband, both of them laughing and smiling in their joy. The duke and duchess were not to depart Northumberland for the continent and the wonderful, jealousy-inducing honeymoon until after the wedding breakfast.

Isla dabbed at her cheeks, unable to fathom that her eldest sister would no longer be living with them. That they would no longer share a room, ride about the estate, swim, and play in the river as they had done so many times growing up.

She was a duchess now, a wife, and no matter how happy Isla was for her, the lump in her throat would not dissipate.

Her younger sister—in Isla's opinion taller and much more handsome than any of the other Woodville sisters—hugged her. They stared wistfully at the ducal carriage as it pulled away from the church and started back toward their home. "Can you believe it, Isla? Our sister is a duchess. The horror of it all."

Isla frowned up at Julia, wondering what on earth she was talking about. "You cannot mean that. Hailey is the happiest, and I daresay one of the luckiest women in England right at this moment. She fell in love with a farmhand and somehow kissed him, and he turned into a duke. Not many would be so lucky."

"Yes," Julia agreed, her tone mocking. "But do you not see? It increases our chances of making grand matches as she did. And I do not know about you, but have you seen the gentlemen here this morning? A lot of popinjays if you ask me."

Isla looked about and pursed her lips. Those in attendance were all very fine and much more handsomely dressed than they all were, even though her family did not lack monetarily. But mayhap, in London next Season, they ought to reside in Cheapside and not Mayfair just to be certain no one realized just how well-situated each Woodville sister was.

"Very well, I agree. They all look terribly dull, but as they are His Grace's friends, we owe him the honor of being kind and speaking to every one of them. It would not hurt, I suppose, not to make enemies of any of them, especially since I'm to have a Season next year, and you will follow me soon after."

Julia slouched. "Urgh, do not remind me. Mama has already expressed ways in which to make me appear shorter. Bar cutting off my legs, I do not see any of her ideas as successful."

Isla laughed, pulling her sister to where the family carriage was waiting. She jumped up without assistance from Thomas, who held out his hand. "No need, Thomas. I'm quite capable, I assure you."

Their old retainer, who had been in their employ for many years, grinned at Isla before helping Julia up. "I do hope Mama and Papa are not long. Mother seems to be making the most of all the London *ton* being here today."

"Well, it is highly unlikely that they will be so again." Her sister Hailey would, of course, host house parties and have to entertain the duke's friends, her friends now too, she supposed, but they would not. They would settle back into their quiet country life and wait for the next London Season. That was enough change that was to come. Now that her sister was a duchess, their ranks had increased, and they would be looked upon more favorably in the *ton*.

Not to mention that because of her mama, once known as Lady Anne, the Earl of Smithfield's daughter and newly returned to take her place in society, they would not escape being thrown into the paths of such as the gentlemen who were here today.

Finally, after a little time, their parents made their way toward the carriage, their smiles making Isla grin. They were so happy for Hailey, and they loved the duke. He had won over all their hearts with his love for their sister. One could not be anything but overjoyed by their marriage.

"Assist me, Thomas," her mama asked as they bustled up to the carriage. They settled across from them, pleased smiles on both their faces. "Your younger sisters have decided to walk home, which I have agreed to since the service was so very long. They will be home in time to see Hailey and the duke off."

"You mean the Duke and Duchess of Derby, Mama," Isla said as the carriage lurched forward.

"Oh, how well that sounds. My dear daughters, you two

3

are next, and I think that since you're such a tall girl, Julia, you shall debut with Isla. You are, after all, twenty next year, and Isla will be one and twenty. A debut together will save money, and we must make the most of your sister's new popularity in town. It will possibly mean you both will make fine matches."

Julia huffed beside her, staring out the carriage window.

Isla knew there was little point in arguing with her mama. When she had her mind made up, there would be little to say or do that would sway her. No doubt she was as headstrong as her father the earl was rumored to have been.

"Let us hope that we find a match that is as loving as Hailey has found. An honorable man who cares for his wife more than anything else. That would be welcome enough for me," Isla added.

"Of course," her father agreed, winking at her.

Isla let the rocking carriage lull her a moment, enjoying the quiet while they had some before the wedding breakfast began.

"I heard that Viscount Billington is holding a house party next week and has been giving out invitations to those at the wedding that he is acquainted with. A house party to celebrate the end of the Season, apparently."

Isla had met Viscount Billington, and he was a pleasant-enough gentleman. However, the idea of a house party with the majority of people at this wedding made Isla shudder in revulsion. She did not want to go anywhere until she was forced to next year.

"Mayhap, you may be invited, Isla."

"Me?" she said, louder than she ought. "Why on earth

would he invite me? I do not even know him all that well, other than the fact he is Derby's friend."

"That is exactly why I would think you will receive an invitation." Her mother sent her a pointed stare. "It would do you good to go, and you may take Molly with you. Now that your sister is a duchess, we must make improvements where we can, and I have hired more staff to help upstairs."

"I will not know anyone, Mama. Hailey will not be in attendance as they'll be traveling to Paris soon. Please do not make me go. I wanted to spend the last of the warm weather at home with my family." Reading and keeping away from everyone, just as she preferred. Not traipsing about England in search of a house party where she knew no one and doubted anyone would pay her any mind without Hailey and the duke being by her side.

"You will be welcomed with open arms, and I shall make sure you will not be ignored if you do receive an invitation. Do not worry, my dear. It will all work out well."

The carriage turned into Woodville House's drive, and glancing out the window, she could see the duke's highly polished carriage parked in front of the house. "How long do you think the wedding breakfast will take?" she asked, not wanting to sound too eager to disappear. Still, the week had been chaotic with her sister's marriage preparations. All she wanted was to curl up on her bed, read her latest novel she had purchased and had posted from London, *The Italian* from Mrs. Radcliffe, and nap whenever she felt the urge.

"Several hours, although I do not think Hailey and Derby will be here that long. They will be traveling to Kent so he may introduce her to his staff and their new home."

From what Hailey had told her, it was impressive indeed and only one estate of many. However would her sister manage so many properties and the London town house? Just the thought of such a position made her head ache. When would her sister get time to read books if she had to order dinner, parties, keep housemaids in hand, and have babies? It was a dreadful bore if anyone bothered to ask Isla. Not that anyone did.

She may enjoy romance novels and gothic tales of spies and highwaymen, but she did not want to live a life of such excitement. A sedate, country gentleman would do her very well. Mayhap Mr. Bagshaw had a brother who could turn his attention to her now that his sibling was married.

Or maybe she could just remain a spinster and not marry at all and have adventure and excitement only in her mind.

TWO

Two weeks later, Isla and her maid were led into a large room of Viscount Billington's grand estate outside of York, her mother's plans to have them attend the house party coming to fruition.

Thankfully, Isla had been able to gain an invitation for her closest friend Harlow York, who was now settling into her own room across the hall from her.

"If you need anything else or require any assistance with dressing or hair that your maid is not able to oblige with, please let us know. We have several lady's maids who are more than competent."

"Thank you, Mrs. Smithers," she said to the house-keeper, ignoring Molly's insulted visage behind the older woman's back. "I shall keep that in mind."

A tall, middle-aged woman, the housekeeper nodded and quietly left the room, shutting the door behind her.

"I will not disappoint you, Miss Isla. You will look the most handsome and best-dressed lady here these next two weeks."

Isla waved her maid's concerns aside. "Do not worry

about what the housekeeper said. You know these houses always bring a certain amount of snobbishness with them. I'm certain we shall muddle along perfectly well."

"And, let us not forget that your sister is a duchess now. There would be few who would treat you unkindly."

Isla smiled and went over to her bed. Her trunk was sitting beside the bed, and she opened it, unpacking the many books she brought and placing them on the bedside cabinet.

"Oh, I can do that for you, miss," Molly said, coming over to her quickly.

Isla waved her away. "I'm more than capable of unpacking my books, Molly. If you would hang my gowns and check that they do not need pressing before the night's events, that would be time better spent, I think."

"Of course."

Isla wandered about the room, looking out the window to the grounds, so unlike their own at Grafton. They had a lawn, of course, and a terrace and even a river that ran through the property, but this estate was something else entirely. Grand came to mind when she glanced out on the vast property.

The sun shone brightly on the pristine lawns. Many gardeners worked in the beds that blossomed with color. The terrace beneath her bedroom window housed several guests. Men and women both were sitting at tables enjoying drinks of some kind and talking amongst themselves.

Isla smiled at the serene view, but her stomach knotted in dread. However would she socialize with these people who were far above her in status? Most of them were titled or children of titled nobility. She was a gentleman's daughter, gentry at best.

Your sister is a duchess. That changes everything.

She sighed, wishing Hailey were here with her now. She could handle herself no matter what situation she found herself in.

The door to her room burst open, and she jumped at the unexpected intrusion. "Isla, are these rooms not the most darling things you've ever seen? We shall have such a relaxing, wonderful time these next two weeks."

Isla took Harlow's hand, smiling at her friend, who all but hopped about with excitement. "I'm glad you're here with me. Would you like to go downstairs and meet our host?"

"Lord Billington? Yes, I suppose we should." Isla led them from the room, entwining her arm with Harlow's. "You know his lordship, do you not? He will remember that we're invited?"

Isla smiled, assuming that he would. "He will remember. He's one of Derby's closest friends, and before Hailey and Derby went off on their honeymoon, he had Lord Billington promise to take good care of us. He will hold to such a pledge. Do not worry."

Harlow sighed. "That is very good then. I feel a little out of place since the invitation was extended to me through you."

"Do not feel like that. I'm glad you're here, and his lordship would not have extended the invitation had he not wanted you to attend."

"That is absolutely correct, Miss Isla."

Isla looked up to see Lord Billington waiting for them at the base of the stairs. She smiled, but her eyes shifted past his lordship to the man standing at his back. The breath in her lungs seized, and her slipper caught on the last stair. She stumbled. Not even Harlow, who grabbed hold of her to stop her fall, could change the trajectory of the stumble.

"Miss Woodville, are you unharmed?" Lord Billington asked, the man behind him coming to her aid and helping her to right herself. His fingers tightened on her arm, lifting her, and fire coursed through her blood.

She shook everyone's assistance off, her face burning and her body humming with some new and odd feeling at his touch. How could she have tumbled down the stairs like some swooning heroine in one of her books?

She glanced about the room, noticing for the first time several other guests, ladies who smirked at her misfortune. Isla raised her chin and smiled at Lord Billington. "I'm perfectly well, thank you, Lord Billington," she said. "This is Miss Harlow York, if you remember, from my sister's wedding." Isla turned and pulled her friend forward, who stood staring at all the upper-class lords and ladies as if she had seen a ghost. Harlow dipped into a curtsy, deep enough to be a bow to the queen.

"Lord Billington, thank you for extending the invitation to me."

"It was my pleasure, of course. Isla is practically family now that she's related to Derby. We've been friends for many years, you see."

"Introduce us." The gentleman who had helped Isla after her stumble came forward, his eyes taking in her every feature. Isla swallowed the nerves that sparked at his inspection. He was utterly unlike anyone she had ever met before, certainly the most handsome man she had ever beheld.

He was tall, taller than even Lord Billington. He had a pleasant smile as if he laughed often and found most things amusing. Not to mention his eyes were the darkest shade of blue she had ever beheld. They took her in, and she wondered what he saw when he examined her. Did he like what he saw, or was she not to his taste?

Please let me be to his taste.

Isla threw that unhelpful thought aside and smiled toward this stranger, waiting to be introduced.

"This is Viscount Leigh. Lord Leigh, this is Miss Isla Woodville, who will be joining us for the fortnight."

His lordship bowed. "Miss Woodville, it is a pleasure to meet you."

Isla dipped into a curtsy, taking the opportunity to inspect him further as he was introduced to Harlow. His legs appeared muscular under his silk knee-breeches. She supposed, like most gentlemen, he rode his horse often and partook in other exercises to keep himself healthy. "A pleasure, Lord Leigh, and thank you for aiding me when I tumbled at everyone's feet."

He laughed. The sound was deep and alluring and made her stomach flutter. Mayhap this country house party wasn't such a bad idea after all. Not if gentlemen like Lord Leigh were present. He was above and beyond handsome, and she could while away her day quite happily if the men were all as handsome as he was.

"We were just heading into the parlor. There is a light supper laid out for us all, and you can wander into the gardens if you prefer. The terrace is just beyond the room. We are not doing too many events today as there are still more guests to arrive," Lord Billington explained as they started toward the parlor.

Isla took in the house, much larger and grander than any she had been in before in her life. She was sure that the entrance hall itself could fit their drawing room and entrance into it. Although she had yet to see her sister's new home in Kent with Derby, she knew it would be of similar standing and opulence as this house was.

The floors glistened with polish. The furniture, the finest design, and the paintings that adorned the walls told of a great family's past while their future walked the halls. It was intimidating, and she felt like she was out of place being around nobility. Her sister Hailey should be here. This was her world now, not so much Isla's.

They entered the parlor, a large room that ran a good portion of the lower part of the house. At one end stood a pianoforte and several other instruments. Fireplaces were adorned with hothouse flowers, and the terrace doors were open, letting in a cooling breeze and an abundance of light.

There were already many people in the room, huddled in little groups and talking jovially with each other.

Harlow came up to her, her face expressing what Isla was feeling inside. "There are so many people here. Do these house parties usually invite what looks to be the entire *ton*?"

Isla shrugged, unsure herself, having never been to such an event before. "If we include ourselves in conversations and be pleasant, I'm certain they will welcome us. I think the fact that my sister is now the Duchess of Derby will help us this fortnight."

"I do hope so," Harlow said, walking before her into the room.

Isla felt a presence beside her and turned to find Lord Leigh smiling down at her. "You look a little startled by all of this, Miss Woodville. Have you never been to a house party before?" he asked, keeping beside her as she headed for an unoccupied settee.

"No, I have not, and I must confess to being a little nervous about it all. Do you know what happens at these events? Is there anything specific that you think I should know?"

He waited for her to sit and then joined her, lounging back on the settee as if this were his own home. He crossed his legs, and his muscular thighs drew her eye once again before she severed her ogling and looked out at the other guests. Several ladies seemed quite interested in her conversation with Lord Leigh already. Was the man a catch and highly sought after?

"The usual. Games on the lawn, cards, and dinner parties at night. A musical evening I should think, and several picnics. I believe we are having a hunt, although more for the ride about the estate than trying to hunt an actual fox. It's not the season for such things. I think you will enjoy your time here," he said, his eyes dipping to her lips.

She swallowed, fighting the urge to lick them just in case there was some piece of food or blotch of some sort he was looking at that she had not been aware of.

Instead, she wiped at her mouth with her fingers, hoping she did not look like a complete foolish twit.

"I'm sorry I did not make your sister and the duke's wedding. I had business in London that I could not get away from, which kept me from attending. I heard it was lovely, however."

"It was a beautiful wedding, and I'm very happy for them both. Before traveling to Paris, they are on their way down to Kent now, to the duke's ancestral home. They will be returning for the Season next year."

"I am happy for them," Lord Leigh said, a wistful smile on his lips.

Isla studied him and thanked a passing footman who handed her a glass of wine. "Well, isn't it a little early for wine?" She smiled, taking a sip of the drink in any case. She glanced about the room and spied Harlow in conversation with two young women of similar age. She seemed comfortable, which pleased Isla. Neither of them was used to such company. They were a long way from Grafton now.

"It is never too early for such beverages, Miss Woodville," his lordship teased, sipping his wine, his mischief-filled eyes meeting hers over the rim of his glass. Isla took a deep breath and tried to relax. While these people may not be whom she was used to conversing with or socializing with, she would not disappoint her family or bring shame to Hailey, who now stood at the top of such social standings in London. She would behave, do as everyone else did, and then return home.

"Lord Billington said we may do whatever we pleased today. So we can explore the gardens and house? Is that allowed?"

"Of course. In fact, there is a highly regarded portrait gallery upstairs. Its prospect also looks out onto part of the prettiest visages of the grounds. If you would like to see it, I could escort you. With your maid, of course."

"Isla nodded, having always enjoyed exploring and finding out tidbits of information pertaining to a place or family. She supposed it came from her love of reading mysteries and gothic tales where there was always something exciting to uncover or happening.

"I would enjoy that, my lord. Thank you for being so thoughtful to me."

"Of course." He gave her an odd look before smiling. "We are friends, are we not?"

Warmth spread through her at his considerate words. She had never had a gentleman sit beside her and be so kind. Speak to her and be interested in keeping her company and entertained. It was a novel thing she had to admit she could get used to. Even though she had not wanted to come to this lofty house party, perchance it would not be so bad. Not if she had friends such as Lord Leigh to keep her and Harlow company.

Several footmen and maids entered the parlor with trays filled with sandwiches, meat, bread, fruit pies, and biscuits. Isla had never seen so much food before in her life, and she was certain that even with all the guests who were here already at Lord Billington's estate, even if every one of them ate something, there would be a terrible amount of food left over.

"Come, break your fast, and then we can explore the house and take in the portrait gallery upstairs. I fear if you do not eat, you will expire upon walking the gallery, for it is terribly long."

Isla laughed and stood. "Well, I would hate for that to occur." She started over to the food and knew Lord Leigh was following close behind. A shiver of awareness slipped down her spine, and she reveled in the feel of it. For the first time in her life, she felt alive, vibrant, and someone's point of interest.

No, she decided. This house party wasn't so bad after all. Not with Lord Leigh chasing her skirts about in any case.

CHAPTER

THREE

Duke walked about the parlor after dishing up a plate of food for luncheon. He stood to the side of the room, allowing Miss Woodville and her friend to converse alone. He could understand her nervousness about attending such a party. The young woman had been foisted into the world of the *ton* through her sister's marriage, and it would be a lot to take in and become accustomed to.

Thrown before men like himself. Men who needed a rich wife to keep the home fires burning. If only his life were so simple as that.

You're a bastard for tricking these innocent ladies into a loveless marriage.

He took the opportunity to see who was in attendance for the fortnight. Lady Francesca Lincoln was here. The poor unfortunate woman resembled his horse more than a prospective wife. His gaze moved on to Lady Susan Craig and Lady Martha Daniels, both of whom were huddled together laughing about something they were discussing. All three ladies were from extremely wealthy families, and all possessed dowries that represented that wealth.

Dowries that he needed. But who had the most was what he needed to find out, and then he could act the besotted, courting fool and marry one of them.

He cringed, throwing a strawberry into his mouth and masticating it until it was liquified. He knew he was a bastard for marrying for money, and had his father not thrown it at anyone he asked to play cards with, he knew he would not be in this position. But he was, and there was little he could do about it.

Duke sighed, knowing he could not blame his father entirely, who, for all his faults, had been kind to him at least. Even if he was an atrocious husband. The thought brought up his mother and his inability to save her from the suffering she endured.

He needed a wife with an abundance of funds to ensure the survival of his ancestral home and the running of the great estate and the London town house while also bringing his mother home. She did not deserve the treatment his father meted out, and he would save her.

He just needed a rich wife before he could act so noble.

Lady Martha noted his interest and sauntered up to him, her mischievous smile something he could become accustomed to. She was pretty, if not a little short for his liking, but she was wealthy and no doubt would come into more money and property when her father passed away since she was his only daughter and anything unentailed may be given as a gift to her. It was a possibility. They were, after all, a close family from all reports.

"Lady Martha," he took her hand, kissing the top of her gloved fingers, "you look utterly lovely today. I hope the drive up to York was not too taxing for you."

"Not at all, Lord Leigh. I'm always up for an adventure."

He raised his brow, noting the husky, seductive quality of her voice. The woman may be moving to the front of his list of three for a potential bride. He laughed, sipping his drink and catching sight of Miss Woodville speaking to Lord Kemsley. Her pinkened cheeks and a smile that seemed to brighten the room made him catch his breath. The woman was beautiful, more so than he had first thought her. Her laugh carried across the chamber, and she covered her mouth with her gloved hand as if a little self-conscious of her amusement. Duke smiled, and feeling Lady Martha watching him, he schooled his features.

"I'm glad to hear it, Lady Martha." He gestured for her to sit beside him on a nearby settee, discreetly watching Miss Woodville as he adjusted his seat. "Have you enjoyed the Season? Are you traveling back to the family estate? It's in Surrey, is it not?" he asked her, wanting her to think he was curious. And he was, in a roundabout way. Maybe not in the romantic way that a lady would prefer, but he was sure they could muddle along well enough together. Just as he could muddle along well with Lady Susan or Lady Francesca.

Would you muddle along with Miss Woodville?

Something told him he would not. Something about the young woman was different from the others here. Mayhap it was because she was only one step up from common. They were, after all, gentry, not nobility, and he did not know much about their financial situation. Her sister marrying his friend Derby did not mean the other sisters were financially acceptable to gentlemen like him.

Men like him who needed blunt to finish what they had started. Especially when he was so close now to hiring a runner to seek the answers he sought.

"Our estate is in Surrey. You have done well to remember. Mayhap after the house party, you could visit us. I know Papa would welcome any gentleman caller. With a wife and daughter to keep him company, I'm certain you can see that he misses more masculine conversation he enjoys at his clubs."

Duke chuckled and took a glass of punch from a passing footman. "Would you like one?" he asked Lady Martha. She nodded and took one herself. He seized advantage of the moment of quiet between them. Their conversation was perfectly acceptable and all that a suitor would discuss with someone they looked upon favorably.

But damn it all to hell, he was bored. She bored him, and he could not imagine years and years of such mundane conversations like the one they just endured. Several other gentlemen had now swarmed about Miss Woodville, and they seemed engrossed in her exchange, and if he were any judge of character, they seemed charmed by her.

What were they talking about, he wondered...

"Do you know Miss Woodville?" Lady Martha asked him, her tone less than warm when Miss Woodville's name rolled off her tongue.

"I met her today. I now know her name but other than her sister marrying my friend the Duke of Derby, very little indeed."

"Yes, what a triumph for Miss Hailey Woodville. She did not even have a Season, and she secured one of London's most eligible bachelors. There will be few gentlemen left for the rest of us if those hidden away in the country come out of their dens and marry those deemed appropriate for us ladies in town. If I may be so bold," she said, glancing up at him with mischief in her eyes.

Lady Martha chuckled, but Duke could hear the scorn

in her tone. Did some of the ladies at this party not appreciate that Miss Hailey Woodville had succeeded where so many others had not? Derby had never been so happy with his match from what he had heard from mutual friends.

"Well, you are now out in the country. If I may accept such conflict is happening between the ladies in London and those out here in the wilds of England, mayhap now is your chance to win over the hearts of men here at this house party." The idea of watching women squabble over gentlemen here would at least make the time in York pass much quicker and be more amusing than a game of charades.

She shrugged, her eyes narrowing on Miss Woodville. "What do you suppose they are talking about? Maybe she's telling them all tales of her life at her father's farm? Do you think they have to feed the horses themselves, or do you think they have stable hands for that?"

Duke cleared his throat, taken aback at the barb. Maybe Lady Martha would not be a good choice. She seemed quite the jealous kind and ready to cut anyone down she saw as a rival. "I think you will have to ask her yourself if you wish to know such things, but I highly doubt what you suggest happens. She seems quite proper, do you not think?"

"A little plain, however, but then the new duchess is no better," Lady Martha drawled.

Duke looked back to Miss Woodville, and his breath caught when he found her watching him. Had she heard what Lady Martha had said? From the disappointment clouding her pretty blue gaze, he could not help but think that was the case.

Lady Francesca joined them, and thankfully their conversation moved away from Miss Woodville and her family. Duke would have to ask Billington what he knew of the family. But if he found that she too had a handsome dowry, she would be added to his list of suitable candidates for his hand.

It was the only way he could move forward. His estate and tenant farmers were thankfully handling things well enough to fund the everyday running of his estate and his London home. But it left nothing for anything else. He would marry one of the ladies here at this house party, and he would ensure the marriage was comfortable and pleasurable enough to keep his wife satisfied. But in truth, he was marrying because he needed their fortune.

Some would say he was a bastard for marrying for such reasons, and mayhap he was one. But it was the only way he could source income for what he needed to do and not take anything from the estates that needed the funds to run well.

He would make it up to his wife. He would be affectionate and kind, and she would never know why he married her and therefore there would be no harm or feelings hurt by his scheming.

CHAPTER
FOUR

After dinner that evening, Isla found herself sitting with Lord Leigh, whom she couldn't help but think of as one of the most handsome men she'd ever met in her life. His striking blue eyes flicked about the room with deadly precision and left several women with blushes upon their cheeks.

The ladies at the house party seemed to enjoy his company, and he was more than affable with them all. He had spent quite some time with Lady Martha this afternoon, the Earl of Daniels's daughter, and she, in turn, seemed quite smitten with his lordship.

His attention turned to Lady Martha once again, and she raised one curious brow as he lounged beside Isla, a whiskey on his knee.

"I think you have an admirer," Isla teased. She knew she should not speak so forwardly with those opposite of her sex. Had her mama been here, she would have surely been scandalized, but there was no one to hear, and she doubted Lord Leigh would gossip about her way of speech, not if his amusement at her statement meant anything at all.

"Really?" he drawled, raising one brow in a way that made her stomach flutter. She bit back her sigh and instead ignored the fluttering within her. "And whom do you suppose is my admirer, Miss Woodville?"

She grinned, making herself more comfortable on the settee too. "Lady Martha." She met his surprised gaze, and not for anything could she stop her inspection of him. His hair was longer than it ought to be, as if he had not cut it in several months, and was now curled about his ears and nape.

His blue eyes swirled with an emotion she could not place, but for the first time in her life, she had an inkling of what it would be like to be the sole recipient of a man's desire. Should Lord Leigh look at her like he did just now, but in a romantic sense, she doubted she would be strong enough to withstand him.

Was that what happened to her sister Hailey? Was the duke able to seduce her with just one look? The heroines in her books certainly succumbed to such masculine wiles. Mayhap there was some truth to all that she had read in the past.

"Are not house parties merely an extension of the Season where ladies and gentlemen alike look for a match? I'm assuming you're not yet out, Miss Woodville?" he asked her.

She shook her head. "No, I'm not. And although everyone is charming and very welcoming here, I would prefer to be home."

"You would?" He sounded genuinely surprised by her answer. "Why?" he asked.

"Well... I'm to have a Season next year, so I don't have to form any sort of attachment here at this party. I'm merely doing my part now that my sister is a duchess, but I would prefer to be tucked up in bed reading to this."

He clasped at his chest. "You wound me, Miss Woodville. Is my company so very dull that you wish to retire already?"

"Not at all. Your conversation with Lady Martha this afternoon was most enjoyable to watch. You play the besotted gentleman very well."

He choked on his whiskey. "What if I am the besotted gentleman? Your tone sounds wanting. Would you mind if my interest was diverted elsewhere?"

Isla started at his question. Whatever could he mean by such a thing? "Not at all. You may do whatever you please."

He threw her an odd look as if he could not figure out her meaning. Was it disappointment she read on his visage? Surely not. He would be the last gentleman on earth who would be upset that she did not come here to chase after him.

After meeting him, though, she found him utterly charming, and if he did happen to divert his interest toward her, she would not shoo him away.

"Pity, there is nothing more amusing than being the center of attention and having multiple, beautiful women fighting over oneself."

She scoffed and covered her mouth when she realized she had reacted out loud. He threw back his head and laughed, catching the attention of several guests.

"I do beg your pardon, my lord. I should not have done that."

"Ah, do not worry, Miss Woodville. I, too, have been teasing and a little too forward with you as well. Shall we start afresh?" he asked her, his mouth in an amused grin that told her he did not mean a word of his apology.

She liked him even more.

"Very well. Although I must say, listening to your conversation with Lady Martha this afternoon, I almost fell asleep. Such lively conversation you Londoners have. You must be well rested most of the time."

He laughed again, and she decided she enjoyed the sound of his amusement. Not to mention two delightful dimples rose on his cheeks when he smiled. Golly, to be the center of his attention, to be the woman he loved, would be a heady thing indeed. Maybe she ought to consider marriage more carefully as her mama wanted her to. If other men in London were as handsome as Lord Leigh, taking one's vows with a gentleman would not be so bad.

Hailey certainly seemed to be delighted.

"I think we're going to be fast friends, Miss Woodville."

"Isla, please, everyone calls me that, and whenever I hear Miss Woodville, I think that my sister Hailey is nearby."

"Isla it is then, when we're not so much among company."

Her name sounded so odd, slipping from his lips in his deep, gravelly tone. She shivered, wondering why he had such a strange effect on her. He was handsome to be sure, and amusing, but he had not attempted anything other than friendship toward her person. That she was all jittery and breathless whenever she was around him would never do. She did not want to become the butt of jokes at the house party as some besotted country chit after the eligible Viscount Leigh.

"And may I call you Leigh?" she asked, wanting to move her mind away from imagining what his lips would feel like against hers. He had the loveliest mouth, his teeth perfectly straight. How providential he was in fortune and status. He

TAMARA GILL

had everything, and while she was lucky indeed herself, she knew as well as anyone that she was not as accomplished as those in attendance here at Lord Billington's estate. She could not draw or play the pianoforte very well. She could read, however, and ride a horse as well as anyone, and so long as no one asked her to sing, all would be splendid.

"You may call me Leigh, of course. Or, since we're becoming fast friends, those closest to me call me Duke."

"Duke?" she asked, wondering how it was that he came to be named so. "People call you Duke?"

"It is my given name. A gift from my father who always thought the family ought to have a dukedom, not a viscountcy."

"Oh dear, your father seemed quite the character," she said.

He cringed a little at her words. "You have no idea," he said before smiling at her, seemingly shaking off any melancholy feelings their conversation brought up.

Isla thought about his name and what she felt most comfortable using. "I think I shall call you Leigh, and then no one can suspect anything untoward between us. I do not wish to cause talk or get in the way of Lady Martha's plans."

"You speak as if using my given name would make people think that we're having an illicit affair."

She choked on her sip of wine and quickly placed it on the small table before them while she caught her breath. "I would never presume to be so forward, my lord. I hope that is not what you think of me." Even though she had imagined his mouth on hers only minutes before and what it would feel like for him to kiss her.

"I'm merely teasing." He poured a small glass of water and handed it to her. "Drink this. It will help."

Isla did as he suggested and felt better for it. "You know as well as I do that to use a given name is looked upon as favoritism and possibly the start of courtship. You should not tease me so with trying to shock me."

"But it is so amusing to see you all flushed and muddled." Their eyes met and held, and Lord Leigh cleared his throat, glancing away. "But I promise not to try to shock you anymore. We are friends, and I like your company. I hope we can spend more time together during the two weeks we're here in York."

"And I too," she said, a little disappointed when he excused himself and went to speak with another group of guests. Thankfully Harlow came and sat beside her, a curious look on her face.

"Was that Lord Leigh speaking to you yet again? I think he may like you, Isla."

She shushed her friend, fighting the urge to look where the viscount now stood, even though out the corner of her eye she could see he was taller than the gentlemen and one lady he stood with. Lady Susan Craig, if she were correct.

"We are acquaintances, that is all. He's merely being polite to me because of my sister marrying one of his friends in town. There is nothing more to it than that."

"Hmm," Harlow said, her tone not convinced. "I beg to differ. He's a viscount, wealthy, and not in need of a wife, but he's here, talking to you."

"And others," Isla interjected. "Even now, he has Lady Susan all aflutter and blushing. I wonder what he is saying."

Harlow looked in his direction, a small frown crossing her brow. "Well, I think he does like you. You merely need to make him like you better than anyone else here. Do you wish to do such a thing?"

Isla shrugged, unsure she did. She was to have a Season next year. It wasn't important she made a match beforehand. And, well, this party was really just so she could meet some new people before traveling to London and having a Season.

Entering the Beau Monde. The fickle *ton*.

"I do not know him well enough to decide, but I'm sure by the end of the house party I shall know if I want to further my acquaintance with the man in London."

"Did you hear that tomorrow we're to partake in a hunt? Although I think it's closer to a ride about the countryside rather than trying to catch the dear little foxes that usually they chase. Will you be going? I heard several ladies are not because the jumps that the gentlemen like to enjoy are too high."

The thought of riding at speed, gaining some fresh air, and looking over this lovely estate was tempting. And she was never one to not go on a ride if offered. "I think I will attend. What about you?" she asked Harlow, knowing she too enjoyed riding horses as much as she did.

"Yes, I think I shall attend," her friend said, glancing across the room and watching Lord Kemsley, a marquess, if Isla was correct. She narrowed her eyes on her friend, wondering at the light blush that stole across her cheeks while watching the gentleman.

"Talking of matches, is there anything that you wish to tell me regarding yourself, Harlow?" Isla inquired, pinning her to the spot.

Her friend's blush deepened, and she sipped from her glass of ratafia, which was unfortunately empty. Isla chuckled.

"No, I have nothing to add regarding myself," Harlow answered, placing down her glass. "I'm merely trying to guide you since a certain gentleman seems to seek you out often."

Isla looked back to where the viscount stood with Lady Susan, and as much as she would like to think he may harbor an inkling of something more than friendship, she would be deluding herself to believe such fanciful thoughts. No viscount, not any of these gentlemen here present would look to her, not when there were so many other ladies of greater social influence than herself to choose from. No, they would be friends, and she would be content with that. At least in London, mayhap he would help her decide on someone suitable and guide her through the many gentlemen who may court her if she were so fortunate to make all her mother's dreams come true and become the latest diamond of the first water.

An unlikely dream, but still, he could guide her such as a brother might do. If she could solidify their friendship here at the house party.

"I am friends with Lord Leigh, and that is all, and that is quite enough. Until we're in London next year, there is no rush to the altar."

"Too true," Harlow said, sighing as if she only half-believed what she had said.

Isla smiled at her and sipped her drink, counting down the hours until she could go to bed and read and then partake in the hunt tomorrow. It was a much more enjoyable way to pass the time than sitting in a drawing room after dinner pretending to enjoy oneself as they were right now.

Dull did not even come close to how bored she was.

CHAPTER
FIVE

The following morning Isla was pleased to find that she was given a mare of sixteen hands. Her horse had kind eyes, which she found comforting, and lovely long legs that would help her get over any hedge groves or fences that they may come across.

Lord Billington had assured her mount was both placid and competent, not that she minded a lively ride, so long as they allowed her to ride astride. Today, if her mount was as they said, she would ride side saddle and look the part of the lady her mama raised her to be.

They set out not long after breaking their fast, and thankfully Isla noted several other ladies had joined the hunt. All of them seemed accomplished riders if the first small fallen tree limb jump they had to cross was any indication.

Isla kept to the rear of the riders, letting those who wished to make sport of the day and race through the course and back to the house have their fun. She wanted to revel in the fact she was outdoors for the first time in days, free to walk or gallop, whatever she chose to do before returning to the house. They may not have another day out like this one, not on the horses in any case. The house party was, after all, only two weeks in duration.

She spied the riders in a field ahead and then heard the steady thump of hooves coming up from behind. She glanced over her shoulder, and her heart stuttered at the sight of Lord Leigh approaching fast. He was too good to be true, the wind whipping at his riding jacket and hair. He appeared determined and strong. The type of gentleman she had only read about in her novels.

She had not seen him in the group of riders readying themselves at the estate and had thought he did not want to take part in the hunt. Perhaps he was merely a little late for the event.

He pulled his mount to a comfortable trot beside her. He wore no hat today, and his hair was a little windswept from his gallop. She drank him in for as long as she could before looking back between her horse's ears.

"I almost missed the hunt. That will teach me not to dally in my rooms longer than I ought."

"You were dallying in your rooms, my lord? Whatever for?" she asked, genuinely curious as to why. He did not look like a man who lay about and ran late for things. On the contrary, he appeared to be engaged and eager for any event that came his way.

"My valet misplaced my riding boots after my arrival, and I had to wait for them to be found. Luckily, they had been left downstairs in his room when he took them down to polish, but I nearly missed the ride. And that, my dear, would have been a tragedy indeed."

"Indeed," she said, unable to hide the grin from her lips. Did he mean that he did not wish to miss riding with her? He was riding alongside her now. Certainly, he seemed to have enjoyed her company back at the house. Was she foolish and too hopeful to want such an outcome with Lord Leigh? To want him to think of her as much as she was starting to think of him?

She met his gaze, his easy smile settling her fears. "I do love a good hunt even though this one is in name only."

"A woman after my own heart," he teased her. "And look ahead, Miss Woodville, for the jump is one of the highest we'll cross today. Make sure you have yourself well seated for it."

Isla looked ahead and saw the hedgerows that grew through an old wooden gate. The hedge had been cut down to the gate level, but even that did little to lessen the height they would have to clear. She adjusted her seat, gripping the reins but allowing more lead to her horse. Lord Leigh made the jump with ease, and she spurred her horse on, leaning forward and low on her saddle to help her horse make the jump.

Except, just as the horse lifted its two front hooves, a fox bolted out from the hedgerows, startling her mount. Mid-jump, her horse shied and landed awkwardly. With little success, Isla tried to counteract her horse's jump to the side, and with dread rising through her, she knew she was about to come off.

The ground came up to greet her with sickening speed, and she landed on her back, the earth only partly softened by the grass. Isla watched as her horse bolted off toward the other riders who had ridden away. She lay there for several moments, each breath she took burned her lungs, and she fought to control the panic that threatened to overwhelm her.

"Isla!" The sound of Lord Leigh's voice went a little way in calming her. He skidded to a stop at her side, helping her to sit up, his hand rubbing her back in a comforting manner. "Are you hurt? What happened?"

"There was a fox," she gasped, trying to get a breath into her lungs.

"You're winded," he said, the circular stokes on her back calming her more. "You will catch your breath in a minute or so. When one lands on their back as you just did, it literally knocks the breath out of you, but you will be well, I promise."

She nodded, concentrating on his soothing voice and words. After several minutes her breathing became easier, and she looked up at him. "Thank you. I've never fallen from my horse before. As much as it was a new experience for me, it is not one that I wish to experience again."

His lordship laughed, taking her hand and helping her to stand. He studied her a moment, his gaze moving to her hair. He reached up, playing with her dark locks. "You have a stick stuck in your hair."

She reached up, and their hands touched. A small smile lifted his lips, and all thought of her fall dissipated. They were standing close, too close. Should anyone come upon them tongues would indeed wag, not that she was in a rush to move away. This close, she could smell Lord Leigh's cologne—sandalwood, and something else that was wholly him. He smelled as divine as he looked. It was no surprise he was a favorite of the ladies at the house party.

His fingers slipped through her hair, and then he held up the stick before her face, proud to free her from the menacing reminder of her fall. "There, it is out, and you are your perfect self once again."

Perfect self?

"Thank you, my lord." She gestured to where his horse

stood. "You may continue your ride if you like. I shall walk back to the estate from here. It is not far."

He frowned, shaking his head. "No, I shall not leave you alone after such a fall. I shall walk with you back to the house. Just let me get my mount to jump over this hedgerow once again, and we will be on our way."

Isla nodded, glad that he chose to walk with her than return to the hunt. She still did not feel the best, and a little selfish part of her wanted him to remain with her.

"Thank you, you're too kind." She stepped out of the way as he jumped back on his mount and glided it over the fence with ease.

She sighed, wishing she had not fallen and was still riding. She had been looking forward to today too. He dismounted and came to her, helping her over the fence before they started back for the estate.

His hand was warm on her arm before he lifted it and entwined hers with his. "I'm sorry to keep you from the hunt. If you were like me, you were looking forward to the day about the countryside."

He waved her concerns aside, seemingly not worried that they were headed back to the house. "It is no mind. I can go for a ride whenever I like. And it would not be right should I leave you on the field to make your way back home. Whatever would Derby think of my atrocious manners should I not escort his sister-in-law back to the estate?"

She threw him a small smile, and yet disappointment stabbed at her heart. He was only helping her out of gentlemanly manners. What was expected of him as a lord and friend to her sister's husband, the duke? She probably ought to forget her fantasies of them riding off in the sunset like so many of her heroines in her books. Certainly, after today it was probably best that she stay off a horse altogether.

"Well, again I thank you. It is never pleasant to fall off one's mount."

"I've fallen off many times, sometimes due to my own inability to stay on top of the saddle."

She laughed, imagining all sorts of situations that may bring on such antics. "Do not tell me, Lord Leigh, that sometimes you imbibe in too much wine and struggle to keep your seat. I can promise you this much," she grinned, "my falling off today was due to a fox, not being foxed, I assure you."

He smiled down at her, his hand coming over hers on his arm and holding her there. Whether he knew what he had done or not, she did not know, nor was she going to ask and have him remove himself from her person.

She liked him. Liked having him touch her.

Her gaze slid to his lips, his next words lost to her as she reveled in the sight of him talking. He was so handsome and kind. He would be the perfect type of gentleman who she would allow to court her. She had not wanted to come to this house party, certainly not a house party with mostly titled gentlemen and ladies whom she had little in common with, but being with Lord Leigh, she could not help but change her mind.

Her Season in town next year would not be so very bad. Certainly not as bad as she had started to think it would be. Not if all the gentlemen at the balls and parties walked in the park, and Almacks was as accommodating and thoughtful as Lord Leigh was.

"I feel like we are becoming fast friends, and you are quite amusing, Miss Woodville. You were so very nervous and serious when we first met that I did not always think that would be the case."

He started down a small hill, and before her, she could see the brook that had been the first jump for the hunting party. "I was nervous, you see, my lord," she admitted to him. "I do not know anyone other than Lord Billington and not even his lordship very well. I was worried that I would not be welcomed here due to not being, well..." She paused, searching for the right words so as not to insult him or his friends.

"As high in the instep as some of the guests here are?" he finished for her, a mischievous light to his eyes. "I can understand your woe, but I think you have settled in well, and I have not heard anything but good things said about you."

But what do you think about me? Isla wanted to ask, but kept her mouth determinedly closed. "Everyone I have met so far seems very nice," she lied, knowing there were several ladies who were yet to speak to her or offer the hand of friendship. She was more than ever thankful her friend Harlow had been allowed to attend with her, so she was never alone. "But yes, my father may be a gentleman, but we live a quiet kind of life to what I think you are all used to. I'm not yet comfortable in this sphere that has opened up to me since my sister's wedding. I feel like the odd one out."

"Well, you do not look to be the odd one out." He held out his hand as they came to the slow-flowing waterway, helping her step on several boulders that allowed her to pass over the brook without getting her boots wet.

"Thank you," she said as they started up the slight incline. Their view opened up to the estate at the top of the small rise, grand with its sandstone walls and glistening windows. The home of one of the largest country estates she'd ever seen before.

"Is your house similar to Lord Billington's?" she asked him, curious to know more about him.

"Ah," he stammered, "a little. My estate is as large, I think the number of rooms is on par with Billington's estate, but the houses are quite a different shape. His is a rectangular-shaped home where mine is U-shaped, with a large, paved terrace that stretches between the buildings. I will admit it makes for disembarking from horses or carriages a much more pleasant experience when there is no mud underfoot."

"So it is similar to Versailles," she suggested.

"Have you ever been to the royal palace? I hear it is quite beautiful."

"No, I have not," she admitted. "But I have seen drawings and would love to visit there one day." Isla wanted to see a lot of places and live life to the fullest just as the heroines in her books relished doing.

"Nor I, but you are right. The courtyard is similar, but by no means as grand."

They came closer to the house, and the drumming of horses' hooves caught their attention. They could see the hunting party travel across the top of a hill in a distant field, riding hard on their mock hunt.

"Thank you for walking me back, my lord."

He tipped his hat, waving her through the front door that a footman had come to open for them. "The pleasure was all mine. I shall see you at dinner, Miss Woodville."

Isla's mood lifted, and she all but floated up the stairs. What a generous, thoughtful man he was. So unlike what she had pictured any of the gentlemen at this party to be. He would be the type of gentleman whom she ought to strive to marry. One who did not think himself so far above her. Not dismissive or rude.

But could she make him see her as a potential bride? They were already friends, and that at least was a good foundation to build on. And she would start tonight, build on that footing, and hope for the best.

CHAPTER
SIX

After dinner that evening, Duke stood in the smoking room with Billington and several other gentlemen staying at the estate. The ladies had retired to the drawing room, and Duke could hear the muffled sound of the pianoforte being played.

"You seem quite enthralled with Lady Susan and Lady Martha, Leigh. Do not forget poor Lady Francesca, or she will have a fit of the vapors from being left out in the cold by your lack of attention," Sir Terrance taunted before taking a long draw of his cheroot.

Duke refused to rise to the man's bait. He had reasons for looking for a rich bride, and no one in his social sphere needed to know the real reason as to why. He did not mind them thinking he wanted it merely to save his estates and to keep him in the affluent life he was born into. They could never know the real reason was to bring his mother home so she could take up her rightful place in their family. No doubt they would find out soon enough. When he located his mother in Spain and returned her to London and her rightful place as the Dowager Viscountess Leigh, then he may explain himself, but until then, they could think the same as everyone else. That he was seeking a rich bride because his father had failed in his duty to the family to keep the coffers full of blunt.

"I have not dismissed Lady Francesca yet, Sir Terrance. The house party is young, and there are many more days yet for me to decide on which lady will suit my needs best."

"Or which one has the largest fortune?" Billington stated.

Everyone laughed, including Duke, and yet he did not find the situation amusing at all. He hated to have to marry for money, to save his family from financial ruin. To place him on the chopping block of an arranged, beneficial, monetary marriage for the rest of his life. He had not wanted a bride under such circumstances, and he loathed the situation in truth.

He swallowed the savage retort on the tip of his tongue and instead shrugged as if chasing fortunes was an amusing pastime he enjoyed. "You know as well as I that the late viscount was lucky to keep the Hampshire Estate and the London town house. I now need enough resources to keep those employed by me and living under my care to remain to do so. I will not end their employment simply because my father did not know how to economize," he lied. Sort of. He needed the funds to keep the houses running and gain a little safety concerning his income. But he needed money to bring his mother home. To withdraw her from Bedlam in Spain would not be cheap. His father never wished for her to return, and he had little doubt it would cost a small fortune to have all records of her being there destroyed.

"Well, I have it on good authority," Lord Kempt said, meeting his eye, "that Lady Susan Craig is the richest heiress at the house party. Thirty thousand pounds at least plus property."

"No, it is Lady Francesca. She will inherit property and has a dowry that would make any man overlook the unfortunate length of her face."

Duke frowned. For all of Lady Francesca's unfortunate features, the lady was considerate and polite, and she did not deserve their opinions on her features, which he had no doubt she was well aware of and probably quite self-conscious of too.

"What about Miss Woodville?" Billington suggested, sipping his whiskey. "Derby did not tell me what his marriage afforded him, but I have heard that all the sisters have the same dowry figure."

"It would be probably five thousand pounds at most, I would think," Sir Terrance said, nodding as if assured of this figure. "You can see by her clothes for a start. Her friend too looks as fashionable as a lady's companion and that leaves me to conclude that neither have much."

Duke frowned. He wished Miss Woodville was worth more than five thousand pounds, but such a small sum would not suffice. No matter how pretty or intriguing she was, he had to seek a fortune to save himself and his family. "Well then, it looks like I shall have to increase my gentlemanly wiles toward Lady Susan if I'm to gain an heiress for a wife. I shall set forth from this evening and double my efforts to win her heart."

"And her purse." Billington laughed. "We wish you well, Leigh."

He nodded, but there was no pleasure in it. He did not want a wife under such circumstances, but he had little choice. He could not in all good conscience allow his mother to rot away in an asylum she did not belong in. She had spent too many years there as it was.

"Thank you," he replied. "But I think a few moments alone with her, and several kisses, and she will be my willing fiancée in no time."

Sir Terrance tipped up his glass in salute. "We look forward to watching your wiles and seeing you accomplish your goals."

And he would accomplish them. He had no other choice but to.

I sla slumped against the wall in the chamber that adjoined the smoking room. She had not meant to eavesdrop but had wanted to look at a family painting that had been discussed at dinner and had overheard the gentlemen enter next door not long after.

Lord Leigh was a fortune-hunting arse! She wished she had not heard his words that spoke of a man determined to marry a woman for her money and not her heart. What a cold, unfeeling type of man to marry a woman for such underhanded reasons.

Of course, she knew that people married for convenience more often than not, but it was not the reason why she would marry and nor would she allow the ladies here at the house party to be fooled by a handsome face and sweet words from a man who did not mean a word of them.

She moved away from the door, trying to be as quiet as she could as she left the room, forgetting entirely about the painting. Not that much held her interest at the house party any longer. Not after hearing that if she were only worth five thousand pounds, she was unworthy of a husband. At least, that was what all of the men discussing the issue with Lord Leigh thought.

All of them, Lord Billington, Sir Dung, and Lord Kempt, deserved a proper set down. But then, if she hollered at them like a fishwife, they would know she had overheard their conversation, and that would never do.

She frowned, entering the parlor just as her friend Harlow finished playing the pianoforte. Several ladies clapped while Lady Susan's visage reeked of distaste.

What foolish men to think she was worth only five thousand pounds. She was worth far more than any of the ladies here. Her family may be gentry indeed, not nobility, but her parents had not lived extravagant lives, and her dearest papa was already more wealthy than most lords in London when he married her mama.

Not that she would tell any gentleman that her dowry was forty thousand pounds, for they did not deserve her or her fortune. But they did deserve her wrath at their greed. They would undoubtedly use the funds to keep a mistress or gamble or enjoy a life of luxury and vice. The women present were probably all here like poor unfortunate souls sold at a meat market.

"Ladies, we hope you have not missed our company too much," Lord Leigh teased, throwing her an amused smile as the gentlemen entered the room.

Isla sat beside Harlow and fought not to glare at each of them. Nor would she allow the hurt in her chest to get the better of her for thinking Lord Leigh more preferable than he was. She had thought him her friend, mayhap even more than that if they could get to know each other more.

"What is the matter, Isla? You're very pale," Harlow said, passing her a glass of ratafia, a concerned frown on her brow.

"If I tell you something, will you keep it between us? I'm still processing it myself, and I will admit that I'm very shocked and disappointed."

"Of course," Harlow said, reaching out to comfort her.

Out the corner of her eye, she could see Lord Leigh bow before Lady Susan. The woman's tinkering laugh grated on Isla's nerves. "I overheard several gentlemen, and Lord Leigh whom I thought highly of, that he is here merely to gain a rich wife. The gentlemen seemed to think it some kind of sport to chase the ladies with sizeable dowries."

"Really?" Harlow said, her eyes going wide with alarm. "What a notion to talk about such things out loud. Of course, we know that gentlemen, and ladies too, I should mention, do seek husbands and wives who may help the other spouse's less-abundant bank balances, but discuss it as a sport? Well, that is very bad manners indeed."

"Indeed," Isla agreed, grinding her teeth. "They were laughing about it, and Lord Leigh was in agreement, mentioning Lady Susan, as they think she is the richest lady among us."

Harlow scoffed, sipping her drink. "Then they are fools, and we know something that they do not."

"Nor will we tell them," Isla mentioned, just in case Harlow took as much offense as she did and talked of what she knew.

"If Lord Leigh finds out that you are worth a fortune, you may become his target. Whatever will you do if he does that?"

Anger thrummed through her at the idea of being courted, flirted with, and spoken to as if she were the most wonderful woman of his acquaintance while knowing all the while it was all false. That she was nothing but a purse to him. She had thought him better than that.

"He will not, and we must hope that no one else here knows what we're worth, you included, Harlow. You are not without a significant dowry."

"That is true," Harlow agreed. "But my dowry is smaller than yours." She paused, watching several gentlemen as they stood talking with the guests. "You were becoming fast friends with his lordship. However will you get along with him now?" Harlow asked her.

Isla pursed her lips, debating that very dilemma. "Well, I will treat him with cool indifference, and I shall ensure that no lady here falls under his spell and is married off merely because she can save his financial concerns." She shook her head, her eyes narrowing on the gentleman she had thought better than he was. Disappointment stabbed at her, and she couldn't help but wonder how many other gentlemen she would meet in London next year who were merely in need of a rich wife.

However would she know before making the terrible mistake of marrying such a cad?

"You are going to stop him from making a match? If he comes to know why you're causing him such strife, he may be unpleasant to you. Are you willing to take such a risk?" Her friend threw Lord Leigh a dubious glance. "I think in a temper he would be quite scary, all told."

"He would do nothing, and nor could he for what I accuse him of is true and came from his own lying mouth. To think I thought him genuine. We must be so very careful, Harlow. There are wolves in sheepskins everywhere in Society."

"Ah, yes indeed." She nodded in the direction of Lord Leigh, who was leading Lady Susan to a vacant settee. "I think you ought to start your saving of these ladies now, if you wish to rescue Lady Susan, that is. I know she has not been the most welcoming to us, but even she deserves better than that."

Isla stood. "She is a woman, and we must combine forces so men such as Lord Leigh do not get away with such underhanded, cruel intentions."

"Good luck," Harlow said.

Isla started toward them with determined steps. It was not she who needed luck. Lord Leigh would need that in spades after she was through ruining all his devious plans.

CHAPTER
SEVEN

uke pulled Lady Susan away from the other guests, wanting to talk to her more and see if she suited him better than the others. If the rumors regarding her dowry were true, she was indeed the wealthiest lady in attendance, and he was sure he could woo her enough to make her want to marry him.

He studied Lady Susan. Her long, golden locks were sun-kissed, and she was fetching. Although their marriage would commence as one of convenience for him at least, that did not mean he would not grow feelings for the lady in time. She was a pleasure to watch as she spoke of her home in London and her family, whom she appeared fond of.

"I have cats too, my lord. I do adore the little animals. They are so affectionate but without being needy like dogs seem to be. Do you not agree?" she asked him.

He paused, wanting to say that cats were opinionated, nettled-type animals that liked to claw furniture and shit in dark corners of homes. That dogs were trainable, obedient, and loyal creatures. Not to mention he was allergic to cats.

Swelling always seemed to occur on his skin whenever one rubbed on his leg or he patted them.

This could prove an issue should they marry and not one he had thought to worry about. "You have cats? Does that mean there are more than one?" he asked, not quite sure he wanted to know the answer to his question.

"Oh yes, I have four. A mother cat, called Mummy Cat, and her three kittens, Ginger, because he's a ginger cat, Torti because she's tortoiseshell, and Black Cat because..."

"The cat is black?" he finished for her.

She smiled, pleased that he had guessed. He stared at her, wondering if she were as bright as he originally thought.

A shadow passed over them, and he glanced up. "Lord Leigh, Lady Susan, may I sit with you?"

Miss Woodville sat beside them and turned to include herself in their conversation without waiting for an answer. "Did I hear you mention that you have cats, Lady Susan? I adore the little creatures, and we have one ourselves at home. He's called Oscar."

Well, at least that is a name... Duke cleared his throat, bringing Lady Susan's attention back to him. "I would like another dog, but I thought to wait until I was married, just in case my bride would like to choose the breed." He smiled at Lady Susan and was pleased to see a rosy hue settle on her cheeks.

"We have a dog too and numerous horses. My sister Julia loves to ride," Miss Woodville mentioned.

Duke narrowed his eyes on her, wondering what she was doing near them in any case. She had not shown to be talkative and the kind of guest who placed herself in other people's conversations before today.

A terrible sensation shivered over him. Was the chit

jealous of his singling out of Lady Susan? Through their friendship, did she think that she had a chance of becoming his wife? He thought on that prospect a moment. Of course, he would have looked at Miss Woodville, hell he would have looked at anyone should they have the funds that he required, but she was not one of them.

He listened to the ladies talk for a few minutes about the menagerie of animals they both owned at their respective homes, and shame washed over him that other than horses, he had not purchased a new dog for the estate which they had always had during the years. What viscount could not afford a good pointer for his estate? Another failing he could level at his father.

"I adore King Charles spaniels. They are the most adorable, and of course, the royal family seems fond of them."

"They are indeed. I think such a dog would suit you," Miss Woodville agreed with Lady Susan. Duke had not thought they had spoken since the start of the house party, but talking of animals seemed to have warmed Lady Susan to Miss Woodville.

He watched the latter, noting the differences between the ladies. Miss Woodville had the clearest skin he had ever seen and a sweet nose that fit her heart-shaped face perfectly. She was an extremely beautiful woman. More so than Lady Susan. Even with all her lofty family ancestors, she still was not gifted with as much beauty as the common Miss Woodville.

Curious.

His gaze dipped to the ladies' gowns and there too were differences. Lady Susan's was of the highest-quality silk and made precisely to fit her form perfectly, while Miss Woodville seemed to favor a good-quality muslin, the gown gaping a little at the bosom. His eyes feasted on Miss Woodville's ample cleavage before he severed his ogling and instead took in the room and the others conversing there, lest she caught him admiring her breasts.

He shifted on the chair, pulling at his cravat. Was the room all of a sudden hotter?

"Are you both looking forward to attending London next year? I hope to see you both there," he said, wanting to move the conversation away from animals. He liked pets as well as anyone else, but there was really only so much one could talk about on the subject.

"Of course, Lord Leigh. My father opens up the London house, which is one of the grandest in London, Miss Woodville. You simply must come to visit me there when you're in town. You would be more than welcome."

Miss Woodville beamed, and he could see she was genuinely pleased to have been invited. "Thank you for your kind invitation, Lady Susan. I would be honored to visit you there."

"We shall go for ices at Gunter's Tea Shop. What a jolly party we will make. Maybe the other ladies present at this house party will join us also."

Duke scrambled with ideas of what to talk about next, but no matter what he interjected, Miss Woodville moved the conversation back to her topic, leaving him out of the conversation entirely most of the time.

He knew when he was bested, and he sat back, listening to their conversation with not a little bit of annoyance, wondering why Miss Woodville would interject herself so forcefully. He thought they were friends. It was odd and not something he thought to witness.

To his shock, the ladies stood and wandered over to another group, discussing plans for the Season and what gowns they wished to order from the modiste. Duke sat, stupefied at having been deserted when his conversation prior to Miss Woodville happening upon them had been going well. Or so he thought.

He needed to at least try to form an attachment to one of the three ladies he had chosen as his prospective bride. He didn't want his marriage to be just one of convenience for him if he could help it. But he had to marry for money, that he could not alter.

The idea of leaving his mother in Bedlam—a place he did not know the conditions of or if she was cared for appropriately or not—for another day would never do. He stood, starting for Lady Martha, the Earl of Daniels's, daughter. Miss Woodville was nowhere near the woman, and hopefully, she would stay where she was so he could see about her being suitable without any interruptions this time.

CHAPTER
EIGHT

The following afternoon Isla saw her next opportunity to step between Lord Leigh and Lady Francesca, who seemed to be having quite the *tête-à-tête* during their stroll about the lawns. She sat with Harlow on a stone bench on the terrace, the scent of wisteria floating through the air and bathing them in dappled light was glorious. Her plan to keep Lord Leigh away from the unsuspecting ladies who did not know he was only after their money also added to the lovely day.

"I watched Lord Leigh last evening, and he looked genuinely shocked that you had slipped yourself into his conversation with Lady Susan. I'm not so certain Lady Francesca will be so forgiving of you if you interrupt them. She seems to not have many admirers."

Which was true, and a pang of guilt ran through Isla at being the one to possibly bring to a close her conversation with his lordship. But better that than have him run off with her inheritance and leave her cold and alone, living a loveless marriage while her husband gambled all her money away at his club.

And possibly other places too that she should not even think about.

"No," she said, shaking her head. "This is for the best, and Lady Francesca will thank me for rescuing her one day. When she's happily married with a brood of children to come home to after balls and parties, she will be indeed happy I stepped between Lord Leigh's courting of her when I did."

Harlow threw her a disbelieving look. "Something tells me that may not be the case."

Isla studied the pair as they walked through part of the garden that seemed to have an abundance of roses growing in it. Lady Francesca pointed out several things in the garden, but Isla could not see what had them so interested from where they sat.

"I will return. Wish me luck." She grinned at Harlow and started toward them. She bit back a smile when Lord Leigh spotted her determined strides, the schooling of his features and tightening of his mouth telling her he was not at all pleased.

Well, he would have to get used to disappointment. For ladies to are displeased and through being pitched into marriages that benefit the gentleman, but not the ladies.

"Good afternoon, Lord Leigh, Lady Francesca. May I walk with you? It is such a beautiful day."

"Yes, of course," Lady Francesca said, a welcoming smile on her lips.

"No, I think," Lord Leigh said in unison to Lady Francesca's answer, his eyes going wide as if he had not meant to say that aloud. "I mean to say," he stammered, "you do not have a bonnet, Miss Woodville. And correct me if I'm mistaken, but do not ladies hate freckles across their noses above anything else? You would not want a set of new ones to sprinkle your skin before the Season."

Isla shrugged, ignoring that he said a new set of freckles as if she already had some over the bridge of her nose. Which she did, of course, but his opinion on the matter was not warranted. "Never mind that, my lord. I'm not one to concern myself with such trivial matters. I have only to worry when it is warranted."

"Really?" he drawled. Isla was not sure she had ever heard anyone sound so uninterested as he did right at that moment. "Do tell us. Lady Francesca and I are curious."

"Well," she started, walking beside them as they traveled down toward a copse of trees that led into the dense forest beyond. "There are many things that I choose to concern myself with. Women's rights, of course, I do think that women and men, no matter their station, ought to have the vote. Sometimes I wonder how our country runs at all without there being a woman in charge."

Lord Leigh snort laughed, and she glared at him, hoping he understood she meant every word that spilled from her mouth.

Lady Francesca, however, arched a displeased brow at his lordship. "What is wrong with women running countries and businesses, my lord? A woman can give birth to a child, which a man cannot. We are resourceful and granted, we may not be as strong in body, but we make up for it more than enough with our minds."

Isla's opinion on Lady Francesca being cold and aloof vanished at the woman's words. She was a bluestocking! How marvelous. "Hear, hear, Lady Francesca. I often wonder how it is that simply by being born a lord, you have the right to sit in the House of Lords. For all we know, a halfwit may be sitting in one of those chairs making decisions on our lives." She shook her head, ignoring Lord Leigh's stunning countenance. "I do not know about you, but I believe that may be the case already. It should not be allowed."

"Lord Flowers comes to mind," Lady Francesca said.

Isla nodded. Although she did not know who Lord Flowers was, she would take Lady Francesca's word on it.

"He fell from his horse and is lucky to be alive. I think he deserves his place at the House of Lords."

"He also drinks in excess and is rarely sober. No, Lord Leigh, I think you are incorrect in your estimation."

His lordship halted, staring at them both as if they had lost their minds along with Lord Flowers. "Since we're being so very honest all of a sudden, do tell me what else you think is worth worrying over and fighting for," he asked Isla, crossing his arms over his chest.

"Well, as for that, I would have to say the unfairness that women face during the Season. Or even at house parties such as the one we're enjoying now."

"How so, Miss Woodville?" Lady Francesca said, a curious tone to her voice.

Isla gestured toward Lord Leigh. "For instance, how do we know if the gentlemen who are here, courting some of the ladies, which we know does occur, are only doing so for their own selfish reasons?"

Lord Leigh narrowed his eyes on her, and she wondered if he had an inkling of where her point was headed.

"Do tell how us gentlemen are here under selfish reasons, Miss Woodville. I'm all ears."

She smiled up at him, and his eyes narrowed farther. "Well, for all sorts of reasons. They may need a wife due to being a widower and in need of a caring hand for their children. Or they may be the sensitive sort who does not wish to be alone. Or, and which is the most common ailment that infects a woman's marriage, she is under the impression that her union is a love match, when in fact, she is merely the means to keep her husband from dun territory. They are the issues I take seriously, my lord. I do not believe any of those could be termed as trivial."

Lady Francesca's laugh startled Lord Leigh from his shocked stupor. "I think we'll be fast friends, Miss Woodville, do come with me and meet my friends." Isla smiled at Lord Leigh as Lady Francesca turned her toward a group of ladies. The sight of his gaping mouth as they walked away was a sight she would never forget. She would best him if it were the last important thing she did in the world.

Before she married a man who loved her for who and what she was. Not because she came with a fortune to line his wanting pockets.

D uke spent the afternoon trying to right himself of the notion that Miss Woodville had an inkling as to why he was at this house party. That three of the wealthiest women in London were here, all searching for a husband was no secret, but that he needed their money was.

His friends knew, of course, how terrible his father had been with the handling of the family financials, but that was only part of the story. His mother did not deserve to be sent away by his father, a jealous man who thought her unchaste. That he did not know if it were true or not, but she was not mad, no matter what his father believed.

He could not allow her to stay in Bedlam in Spain.

Tonight the house party had moved to the large drawing room upstairs, and servants had hung lanterns about the gardens to give the night a magical feel from the view above. The drawing room had a long balcony that the guests could stroll while also sitting indoors to play cards or listen to the pianoforte. The sound of Sir Dung singing a duet with Lady Martha did little to improve his temper.

He cared for none of it. He sat outside in a position that gave him a view of the room and one guest in particular. The one he wanted to strangle.

Miss Isla Woodville.

He ground his teeth. She had to know. Had someone told her of his plight? He frowned, not liking that any of his friends here would out him in such a way to the ladies, but then, he supposed, when such large fortunes were up for grabs, each to their own. All is fair in love and war.

He rolled his shoulders, finishing the last of his whiskey before placing the glass on the railing. Miss Woodville was engaged with most of the ladies present, going from group to group, a complete alteration to how she had been when she first arrived. He had thought she would not socialize at all or meld into the group of women, most of whom ruled the beau monde, but here she was, one of them, accepted and liked.

And keeping him from getting to know the ladies he wanted for his wife. Which one he could not say at present, and he doubted he ever would be able to decide if Miss Woodville kept sticking her nose into his business when it was no concern of hers.

He turned and looked out over the gardens, forcing a calming breath. The hairs on the back of his neck prickled, and he rubbed his nape. A light, airy voice sounded behind him, making his hackles rise.

"Lord Leigh, are you enjoying your evening? You are all

alone out here and are not inside enjoying the affluent company."

Affluent? The chit had to be on to him. "I would prefer to remain outdoors and alone." He wanted to cut her with his words, but instead of insulting her, she chuckled, the sound husky and low. It sent a trigger of annoyance through him along with something else he would not admit to. He wanted to punish her for her impertinence. To interrupt conversations she was not part of was beyond rude. Her actions reeked of her common upbringing. But how to make her pay?

The thought of laying her over his knee and spanking her arse sent heat straight to his groin. He closed his eyes, his fingers tightening on the railing lest he reach for her and carry her off on his shoulder like some heathen.

"Are you angry with me, my lord? I hope I have not offended you in any way."

Her words were as sweet as the wine, but she did not fool him. He turned, staring down at her, and fought not to do what he had imagined a moment ago. She raised her determined chin, defiance lighting up her blue eyes. Little minx knew exactly what she was doing...

"I could ask the same of you. But perhaps it is not anger that you feel toward me, but jealousy. Is it because I have not singled you out that you're hurt by my denial of you, and therefore you are trying to halt any affections that may grow between other ladies of our party and me here?" he asked her, knowing he would never tell her the whole truth. To do so could ruin him completely, and then he would be unable to marry anyone. To have someone in Bedlam was the worst of family skeletons. No one wanted to have children if madness ran in the family's bloodline. Best that she think him a fortune hunter and nothing else.

"I am not jealous, but I did think you were different from any of the other gentlemen here. I was wrong in that estimation. You are just like the rest of the rakes in town, a road full of pits and divots that we ladies must cross without falling into and ruining our silk slippers."

He blinked, unsure what the hell her analogy meant. "Are you trying to say that we lie, madam and that you fall for our tricks?"

"Do you not? Each time you speak to Lady Francesca or Lady Susan, are you really interested in what they're saying, or are you just saying all the right and pretty things that ladies like to hear? As if we're halfwits who have no brain between our ears. You know we can hold a conversation that includes more than lace and modiste visits or the latest on dit. We read and are educated just like you and should be allowed the same opportunities.

"I'm certain we could reach great heights should we be treated as equals. But you, no. You do not care for any of that. You merely wish to tell us frivolous things to make us think you are sensitive and will be a great husband, and yet like so many in the past and future I would suspect you will be a disappointment once the vows are spoken."

Duke had never been given such a set down, and certainly not from a chit who was not his equal. He walked past her, brushing her shoulder with his, and moved away. Better this way than wrenching her into his arms and kissing the wench until she forgot all about her bluestocking ideals and remembered why men and women managed so well together, no matter what pretty things were said by the men before.

"I see that I am correct in my assumption." She laughed behind him as if she had won their little quarrel.

"I can assure you, Miss Woodville, that no matter how I

may have my wife fall in love with me, no matter for what reasons I enter the marriage state for, I can assure you that my wife will never stray from my bed and will be well pleased having entered the marriage state. So I would advise that you stop your games of dropping into other people's conversations and keep yourself away from me. I would hate for us to have a falling out."

Not that he wanted to have a falling out with Miss Woodville. She was like a breath of fresh air in his normally stale life. It had been a long time... In fact, never had he debated with a woman and with one who seemed determined to halt his courtship toward heiresses.

She had to know he needed the funds. There was nothing else to explain her anger.

"I cannot do that, my lord. When I see an injustice like marrying a woman for her money, which I know is your intention, I cannot allow such a travesty to occur. The ladies deserve more."

"The ladies know that is how it is done in our society. But perhaps because you are gentry and not nobility and have not lived in our social sphere, you do not know how things are done."

"Really?" She raised one mocking brow. "I may not be nobility, but at least I will marry for love, not money."

"That is irrelevant. My wife, no matter how marriage to me will come about, a marriage of convenience or not, will not go without. Not in any aspect," he said, leaning toward her and lowering his voice.

Her mouth opened on a small gasp, and his attention dipped to her lips. She was a beautiful woman, and they were alone in the shadows on the balcony. He could easily steal a kiss, give her a taste of what his wife would enjoy, and often. He was certain that any financial transaction made between his family and hers would be soon forgiven when she was pleasured by him.

"I do not understand your meaning, and I do not think no matter what you offer your wife, when she realizes she has been duped into a union solely to save your financial hide, she will be heartbroken. I will not allow that to occur to these ladies. They are my friends."

He scoffed, stepping back. "You are a fool if you think any of these ladies would do the same for you. They know how society works. They are here for reasons just the same as me. Maybe not for money, but a title, a dukedom, a marchioness title, or viscountess such as my wife will be gifted. Do you not see, marriage is a transaction and nothing more? If you wish to be a success in London next year, you ought to lose your delicate sensibilities. They will crush you and make you a bitter old wallflower. But mayhap you already are."

She stormed up to him, her defiant chin making his hands itch to clasp it and hold it steady as he devoured her mouth. Damn it, she was beautiful and more so when she was angry like a little raging inferno.

"I am not bitter, but you certainly make me feel the emotion toward you with what you're doing. The ladies here deserve to know that you're marrying them for their fortunes and nothing more."

He crossed his arms over his chest, merely to stop himself from wrenching her against him. Her breasts rose and fell in her temper, and it was a struggle to keep himself from ogling them or wanting to slide his tongue along the pert, white flesh that taunted him.

"I'm certain they already know that, Miss Woodville. Your efforts will be in vain. The lure of having a title will outweigh any insult they may feel for me regarding their fortune. And anyway," he continued, "why such the uproar? You do not know why I need the funds, and I would also like to know how you came to know of my circumstances?"

"Well, as to that, I overheard you all boasting about certain ladies' fortunes the other evening. The way you discussed your choices based on their worth is despicable, and you ought to be ashamed of yourself."

He chuckled. "Believe this if you do not believe anything else that is said between us, Miss Woodville. I will make my choice based on their income, for, unfortunately, I have little choice in the matter. But I will not be shamed for doing so. Nor would I allow my wife to be shamed for chasing a title. It is commonplace in our society. That I have caused you offense once again brings me back to believing you're jealous that I am not courting you. If only you had a fortune, then you would not be so safe."

She blustered at him, looking even more beautiful than before. "You would court four ladies at the same time merely to see who was more agreeable financially to you?"

"Of course. I would need to know who was worth the most. Do not forget that," he added, wanting to get under her skin a little more. Her mouth gaped, and he leaned toward her, feeling the disgruntled breath on his lips. "I may also steal a kiss or two to see who reacts to my touch more than the rest. That is important."

"Important," she said, her words breathless.

He nodded. "Well, yes, of course. I do not want a cold fish. No matter the basis of that union, a passionate marriage would be preferable. I want to desire my wife. I want her to want me too."

Her gaze dipped to his lips, her eyes growing heavy with desire. He could recognize it on anyone. Not that he would give this hellcat what she wanted. What he wanted too, not that he would admit to such a thing, but damn she was making it hard.

"Women are not as promiscuous as men."

Unable to deny himself, he tipped up her chin, making her meet his eyes. "Oh, Miss Woodville, yes they can be," he said, letting her go and counting the steps toward the drawing room. If he stayed outdoors with her a moment longer, he would show her exactly why women could be as passionate as men and prove her wrong.

He sought out Lady Martha, having not spent as much time with her as the other two. For the remainder of the night, he fought not to glance in Miss Woodville's direction. He could feel her eyes on him, but she would not do. Her dowry was too small. Five thousand pounds was not enough. Even if he had a sinking feeling she would be more than enough for him in every other way.

CHAPTER
NINE

The following day and evening, Isla was able to keep away from Lord Leigh and his opinionated, insulting ideals on why marriages as the one he sought would suit him above any other type.

However, that did not mean that she would allow his ambition to succeed, even after he told her such marriages were commonplace. Lady Francesca, Susan, and Martha were already ladies by birth. They did not need a duchess or marchioness title. Their position in society was already well placed. And if they did wish to gain such lofty marriages, they ought to be allowed to acquire one that included love and affection.

They would be happier in their lives if that were the case.

She wandered from the group who had settled down for cards, several tables laid out in a variety of games for the evening. Such pastimes had never interested Isla, and she barely knew how to play whist, nevertheless losing her pin money by taking part in piquet.

The night was warm, and she slipped onto the terrace,

heading toward the gardens. Again they were lit with an array of lanterns, making the gardens appear magical. In the darkness, a wooden garden structure with wisteria growing over it rose before her. It was circular in shape, and white flowering roses were planted at its base. It was rather lovely, and she knew several ladies had spent the afternoon within it reading and enjoying the shade on the warm afternoon days they were enjoying.

She stepped within and spied several lounge chairs, pillows, and blankets laying over them, just imploring anyone who wanted to laze the day away to enjoy the comfort they offered.

Isla sat on one, lying back and closing her eyes, breathing deep the sweet, lovely scent of wisteria. In the distance, she could hear the mumbled sounds of laughter and music as the house party enjoyed their evening of gambling and cards.

For a time, she lay there, content to remain outdoors for the rest of the evening when the sound of determined foot-steps crunched on the gravel pathway outside. She frowned, a prickle of regret running through her that she had left the party alone and had not told anyone of her whereabouts. What if it was a highwayman intent to rob the estate?

She was about to flee when the recognizable face of Lord Leigh poked about the opening. His annoyance was plain to see, and she sighed, not in the mood to tolerate any more of his opinions. "Oh, it's you," she said, annoyance layering her tone.

"Are you trying to be molested, Miss Woodville? What are you doing outside on your own at this time of the evening? Unless," he said, gesturing toward the gardens.

"You have a rendezvous with a gentleman, and I'm merely delaying the actuality."

He glared at her, and she rolled her eyes. "I do not gamble and wanted to go for a stroll. I'm within sight of the house. I'm perfectly safe," she lied, having only a moment before regretted her choice of slipping away.

Not that she would tell him such a thing. She studied him, so arrogant and lofty. But also, so utterly handsome and dreamy. The kind of rough, coarse gentleman who saved the heroines in the novels she loved to read.

Tonight, he wore a superfine coat, his knee-high silk breeches glistening against the moonlit sky. He was the complete London gentleman, highly starched cravat and jacket that fit him like a glove. He was a viscount, a gentleman with so much more than many, and he looked as if he knew it.

Never in her life before had she ever wanted to wipe the haughtiness off his visage. As if he knew better than her. As if his opinions were worth listening to and obeying. She had never been one to be told what to do, and she wouldn't start with the man before her who had no moral compass.

"You are not safe, not in London or in the country. To wander away from a party such as the one indoors could lead you into a danger you could not imagine. Do not think that people wishing to harm others do not do so here in York. They do and more often than you would ever know."

"Really," she sighed, standing, having had enough of his lecture. "Do you never tire of listening to your own voice, my lord? I came outside for quiet before retiring. I do not need you here rescuing me like some woman who cannot look out for her own wellbeing. Are there not ladies indoors who you believe wealthier than me who would like to listen to you all evening? I am not one of them."

A muscle worked in his jaw, and he stared at her. The pit of her stomach churned, not in a lousy kind of way, but in a way she had never experienced before. It was similar to last evening when she had confronted him on the balcony, but more potent. She would say desire was what she felt if she didn't know any better.

She glared, forcing the idea out of her mind. No, she did not feel desire for Lord Leigh. He was a fortune hunter, and she did not need him to know that she had one. She would never marry a man merely to save his own arse.

Never would she allow herself to feel anything for the man before her but contempt. They may have been friends, but not anymore. She could not be so with someone who would lie merely to get his own way.

"Are you not?" he asked, stepping into the space with her. The area, which she had thought large enough for several people, now seemed small and confined. She met his eyes and stared back, not willing to recoil at his attempt to overwhelm her with his presence. "Why do I think that is not that case?"

"Excuse me," she stated, but even to her own voice, it sounded too high and panicked. "I am not interested in you. Not even as a friend. That ship has well and truly sailed, my lord."

"Hmm." He was before her now, tall and masculine. The scent of the flowers, his cologne of sandalwood she would later blame for what she did next, but in truth, she had crumbled like so many women before her, and it was disgraceful.

Isla smirked. "Are you trying to change my mind, my lord? You will not be successful," she teased, wanting him to try. At least once. To be here with a man she was determined to loathe for all eternity was absurd. But so to would be giving up the opportunity to taste his lips just once. She could hate him after tonight, but for five minutes, what would it hurt to allow him to try to persuade her that he had won this war?

"I think I could. May I?" he asked.

"May you what?" she questioned, her skin prickling in awareness, her legs shaking with need. For a moment, he did not move, and when he did, she wasn't sure her taunting was such a good idea after all. He lowered his lips, brushing hers, so soft and slow as to be painful with the want he ignited in her.

She shouldn't want to be kissed by him, but neither did she want to miss this opportunity to enjoy her first real kiss. And by someone who knew what he was doing. The breath in her lungs hitched, and her mind reeled. He was all warmth and tasted of brandy, of vice, and everything she should not want.

But she did. More than she dared to admit.

***

Duke teased her lips with his tongue, a little part of him wanting to frighten the mouthy chit who seemed to have an opinion on everything he intended to do. He already knew marrying for money was not ideal, but he had little choice. And now, she would pay for her ire toward him, her words that made his skin prickle with guilt.

She gasped, and he deepened the embrace, slipping his tongue into her warm, inviting mouth. She did not pull away. Instead, she swayed toward him, her hands fisting the lapels of his coat, holding him against her.

His mind reeled, a headiness settled low in the pit of his stomach. She was quick to learn, and he angled her head, allowing him to deepen the embrace. The feel of her tongue, tentative at first against his, made him groan. Yes, this is what he wanted. He wanted her to want him as much as he had wanted her these last few days.

Even if she were a little prickle in his boot, kissing her now was payment enough for having to endure her bite. He cradled her face in his hands, moving from side to side, taking her mouth in a kiss that was no longer soft or beckoning but brutal, a statement that she ought not to play with him.

Not in this regard. She did not seem to grasp the danger.

He wanted to touch her but denied himself the need that coursed through his blood. To do anything but kiss her was dangerous. He could not marry Miss Woodville. She may have a dowry, but five thousand pounds would never be enough.

The realization brought him out of his haze of desire. He lifted his head, staring down at her, not quite understanding what had happened between them. She looked as dazed as he felt. Her lips were swollen, her eyes heavy with hunger.

She looked ravished. At some point, his hands had slipped into her hair, knocking out several pins. His attention dropped to her long, brown locks, longer than he had thought them to be. The woman was beautiful, sensual, and utterly captivating.

You cannot marry her...

He stepped back, rubbing a hand across his jaw. "Apologies, Miss Woodville. I overstepped my bounds."

She reached up, pinning her hair as if his words and his kiss were long forgotten. He frowned. How did she compose herself so well, and so quickly? His heart still beat too fast, the blood in his veins going directly to his groin. If she only looked down, she would see what she did to him.

"Do not apologize, Lord Leigh. I kissed you back, as much as it frustrates me that I allowed you such liberties. But, at least I now know what all the fuss is about when a man kisses a woman. I had often wondered, and I have no need to wonder anymore." She slipped past him. The scent of her perfume, fragrant wisteria, floated in the night air. She smelled divine and felt the same in his arms. "Goodnight," she threw over her shoulder as if he were an afterthought.

Duke gaped, shaking his head to clear its fuzziness. Had she really just discharged him so easily? The woman either loathed him as much as he had thought she did or was one of the best actors in England.

He watched her make the terrace and slip indoors. Next time he supposed, he would just have to make their kiss unforgettable and her less presentable. An amusing way to pass the time before he married his heiress and let Miss Woodville marry a man she loved and he in return, leaving everyone satisfied.

The thought of her married to some unknown gentleman left him cold, and he started back toward the side of the house, not willing to enter via the terrace just in case someone noticed him. It was just because the night had turned cool, he told himself.

A lie, but one he would tell himself in any case. Miss Woodville was for someone else and not him, and that was the end of the matter.

CHAPTER
TEN

Isla tossed and turned in bed later that night. The memory of Lord Leigh's mouth on hers, the delicious slide of his tongue against her own made the pit of her stomach clench, and a pleasant thrum occur between her thighs.

She sighed, knowing such thoughts would never do. She hated what he stood for. He wanted an heiress, something she was, not that the fool knew, and nor would she be the one to tell him. She would never marry a man because he needed her money. She liked herself too much to settle for anything less than what she deserved.

The memory of his shocked visage when she had left him in the gardens made her grin. Her dismissal of him had taken all her power to say. When, what she had really wanted to do was wrap herself in his arms, push her aching breasts against his chest and let him do what he would with her. Kiss her more and guide her toward the blissful path he ushered her along.

No wonder women fell from grace when around rakes.

She could certainly see the temptation now that she had kissed one.

She rolled onto her back, staring up at the ceiling, not that she could make out much in the room, other than dark shapes and the windows with the moonlight coming through the curtains.

Isla threw back the covers and lifted her night rail from the end of her bed before leaving her room. She would find a book in the library, one she had not read before, to help her sleep. Lord Billington may even have the first install-ment of *The Moor* by Rosa Matilda, who always wrote stories of strong women who followed their passions and beliefs.

She made her way downstairs and entered the library with soft footsteps without waking anyone. It was thank-fully empty, and she walked over to a wall sconce on the chimney breast and lit the candle to offer light. An array of bookcases came into view, and she strolled along each one, looking to see if Lord Billington had what she wanted to read.

The sound of feminine giggling and a man's deep growl made her jump, and she raced over to the candle, snuffing it. For a moment, she stood in the dark, hoping whoever it was who was running about the house at this hour would not come into this room. Hearing nothing more, she crept over to the door, peering out into the vacant foyer. She couldn't see anyone, but she could hear the muffled sound of a couple having a midnight tryst.

Isla bit her lip. Who was it running about? Was it Lord Leigh partaking in a tryst? She pushed the annoyance that ran through her at the thought and followed the sound, needing to see for herself.

She did not know why the idea of Lord Leigh having a

wicked rendezvous with another woman aggravated her more than it ought, but it did. At least if she found out who it was, Lord Leigh or not, she would know to keep well away from him regarding future courtship.

She pushed the library door open just enough for her to slip through and tiptoed to where she could hear whispers and more giggling. Whoever they were, they seemed to be enjoying themselves. As she walked past the staircase, a hand shot out, startling her. A hand wrapped about her mouth, stifling her scream before a heaving muscular chest came up hard against her back and whispered words against her ear that sent her wits to spiral.

"What are you doing, Miss Woodville? Is it not past your bedtime?"

She bit his hand, and he yelped. The voices in the other room stopped talking, and with a muffled curse, Lord Leigh hoisted her into his arms and carried her into the small closet beneath the stairs. Little light entered the space, but she knew he was facing her.

"Shush," he said, as the sound of footsteps came out into the foyer before they moved on and a door closed deep within the bowels of the house.

"What do you think you're doing?" she demanded of him, his highhandedness reproachable. "You cannot drag me in this room and think it appropriate."

"When you're about to ruin a couple possibly on the verge of an understanding, I can. And anyway, what are you doing about the house at midnight? Mayhap you are loitering about the house in search of a lover."

She narrowed her eyes, even though she knew he could not see her. "I could not sleep. I came downstairs for a book and happened to hear giggling. I was merely going to look and see who it was."

"So you're into watching other couples then. Interesting."

She pushed at his chest, immovable as the oak trees that grew on their estate. "Do not be so crude. Being nosy is not whatever it was you said." She paused, his scent of sandalwood and something else she could not place making her head spin. "I thought it may have been you, and then what I think of you would have been correct after all."

"How disappointed you must have been to discover it was not me." He sounded as if he were laughing at her. She ground her teeth.

"And you, my lord. What were you doing about the house? Mayhap another giggling lady is waiting in one of the rooms, despondent for her Lord Leigh, who has been waylaid by Miss Woodville."

"Do you always talk about yourself in the third person? How strange you are," he mocked.

She felt him step closer, his warm breath tickling her neck. When had he bent his head so close? She allowed the shiver of awareness to slide down her spine, but that was all she would permit. There would be no more kisses. No more anything with this rake. "When the need arises, yes, I do."

She knew he was smiling. She could feel it, and yet he did not say a word for a moment. "Are you jealous if another lady was waiting for me?"

Isla rolled her eyes. The man was insufferable. "If I have not said this already, let me say it again, Lord Leigh. I dislike you. You are everything a well-bred young lady dislikes in a man. A rake to his very core and a fortune hunter too. Not much to admire, I think you would agree."

"And I dislike you, Miss Woodville, and your lofty, judgemental opinions."

She pushed at his chest, little good it did her, for he did not shift. "You are so rude. I do not know why I stay and listen to you."

"And I do not know why it is that I keep finding you in odd places about the estate."

"Are you accusing me of untoward activities?" she gasped, outraged. Being in a cupboard under the stairs was untoward, but it was not planned. Though, in truth, she enjoyed arguing with him. It was amusing to get under his skin. If she succeeded, she might give him a conscience. "If I were doing anything inappropriate, I can assure you it would not be with you."

He laughed, not caring who heard him. "You have already been such with me, Miss Woodville, or have you forgotten my kiss so easily."

"What kiss?" she retorted. "Is that what your attempt in the pavilion outside was? I had thought you were merely trying to drown me with your tongue."

He took a long, slow breath. "Well, I never," he stuttered, stepping up against her. She shifted away and came up hard against the wall. "Are you lying to me? I did not know you as a woman with such a devious tongue."

"I never lie. I always tell the absolute truth," she answered.

"You frustrating minx. You will not relent, will you?"

"No," she said, lifting her chin even though she knew he could not see her. "Not for you in any case."

Duke growled, his body alight with need, with frustration and annoyance at the chit before him. How dare she say he almost drowned her with his tongue.

The kiss they shared outside had left him reeling for hours.

Even now, all he could think of was doing it again.

He slammed his mouth against hers, ignoring the startled gasp he drew from her. He expected her to slap his face. To push against his chest, to scratch his cheeks, but she did none of that. Instead, she clasped his jaw, holding him against her, thrusting her tongue into his mouth with an expertise that left him reeling.

He groaned, taking the opportunity to press his body fully against hers. She met him halfway. Her sweet, womanly curves his to enjoy. He clasped her arse, squeezing the soft flesh in his hand. She was delicious.

His cock, as hard as a rock, pressed against his breeches, and he pushed against her. She moaned, nipping at his lip through the kiss, and he almost spent in his pants. "Damn it, Miss Woodville."

"Isla," she breathed against his lips, her hands splaying about his neck. He hoisted her against the wall, settling her legs about his waist, and teased them both with what they wanted.

"I want to do untoward things with you, Isla," he teased, kissing her cheeks, her chin, her pretty, soft neck.

"Yes," she agreed, rubbing against him like a cat. His mind reeled, and he fought to control himself. She was not a woman he could ruin. Not a woman he could marry. He should not be here, taunting her, all but moments from screwing her, but nor could he break from her touch.

He set her down and worked her shift up to gather at her waist. *Stop, Duke, this is wrong.* He dipped his hand between her legs. So wet and warm, the scent of sex mixed with her sweet perfume muddled his mind further.

He slid his hand over her mons, pressing between the

lips of her sex. "I want to make you shatter in my arms, Isla. Do you understand what I'm saying?" He rolled his finger over her engorged nubbin, eliciting a startled gasp from her.

He felt her shake her head. "No, but I'm certain you're about to tell me."

Duke narrowed his eyes on her, defiant to the very end. She would be the end of him, the little minx. "You're wet and ready, aching for me. Admit that my touch makes you feel wicked."

Her hand fisted in his hair, pulling him close. "Just because I enjoy your petting does not mean that I like you any more than I did before," she gasped when he delved farther along her sex, teasing her core and where he wanted to be right now more than anywhere else in the world.

Duke closed his eyes, reveling in the feel of her, the wetness that taunted him to taste and kiss her to climax. He rolled his finger about her opening, and she moaned against his lips. Their tongues tangled, mating in their mouths. He fingered her, seizing her in the way he wished his cock was right at this moment.

So damn good. He sucked in a startled breath. So tight and wet as she clamped around his finger. Fantasies overtook his mind—ripping his front falls open, hoisting her onto his cock, and fucking her until they were both a pool of satisfaction.

He adjusted his finger, pressing against her in a way he knew the ladies enjoyed. Her startled intake of breath, the undulation of her hips as he fucked her with his hand was too much.

"Lord Leigh," she panted, her hands clutching at him as if to keep her rooted to the spot. "I want," she stammered. "I want..."

"I know what you want," he said, pressing down on her clitoris while he fingered her. Tremors engulfed his hand, and she moaned his name, the sound bliss to his ears. He took her lips, silencing her cries, and let her ride his hand as the last of her convulsions rocked through her.

They stood there a moment, both catching their breaths before Duke lifted his hand from her sex and settled her shift back to rights. He could feel her glaring at him, and although he knew he had given her pleasure, he was not fool enough not to know she would be mad about that now. She did not like him, and she certainly did not appreciate that she liked what he did to her.

She pushed at his chest, and this time he moved away. "Thank you for whatever it was that just happened, but know this, Lord Leigh, it will not happen again."

He bit back a grin as she opened the understairs door, a slither of light illuminating the space. Duke sucked in a breath at the sight of her. Her nipples were taut and beaded through her shift and night rail. Her hair was mussed as if she had been thoroughly bedded.

A fragment of pride and possession ran through him that he had made her lose control. That he had brought her to her first orgasm. The thought of her being so in another's arms made his jaw clench. He did not like the emotion that rose within him, knowing that one day she would belong to another. Another man who was not him.

"Pleasant dreams, Isla," he said, enjoying the inhale of air his words brought forth in her. Still, she was affected by him, and God knows he was affected by her. His cock stood to attention, begging for her touch. She closed the door, leaving him in darkness, and he chuckled. Minx to the very end. However was he to keep his hands off her when all he wanted was to chase her pretty skirts, kiss, and make love to her whenever they desired?

He must. That was all there was to it, he reminded himself, knowing deep down he wouldn't follow his own decree. Not a chance in hell.

CHAPTER

ELEVEN

Isla could not leave her room the following morning until the blush that had plagued her all night, and each time she thought about what Lord Leigh had done to her beneath the stairs eased. His touch sent goosebumps to rise on her skin. Her body ached in places she had never known before. She'd never felt so wanton.

She never reacted to men the way she had with Lord Leigh. That it was the very man she had agreed to loathe for all eternity was not to be borne. She didn't want to react to a man who hankered for women only with the means to save him from debtor's prison. Not that she knew his financial strains were as severe as all that, but they were obviously not good. Not that he had divulged such secrets to her last night.

Oh no, instead, he had distracted her with his clever hands and mouth. Well, not again. She had to keep those who would fall for his charms safe from his fortune-hunting claws.

"Isla, whatever are you doing? You'll wear out the carpet if you keep pacing the way you are."

The sight of Harlow at the threshold of her door pulled her up short, and she sighed, knowing she had to tell her. Had to tell someone what she was doing before she expired with pent-up frustration.

"Shut the door, Harlow. I need to speak to you."

Her friend did as she asked, a worried frown appearing on her brow as she quickly came to her. "Whatever is it? You look upset."

Isla threw up her hands in despair. "I am upset. I'm mad at myself and Lord Leigh for being a proficient rake." She chewed her lip, meeting her friend's startled eyes. "He cornered me last evening. I was, I grant you, snooping on another couple whom I just happened to come across, and he pulled me into a closet so we would not be seen."

"A closet?" Harlow sounded all too calm, and Isla regarded her a moment, wondering how she could remain so unruffled with such an admission.

"Under the stairs. At first, it was to keep us from being caught not only together but to not let the other couple know we had heard them. We argued, not for the first time since the man is a terrible bore, as you well know, but then he kissed me again and I—"

"Again!" Harlow clasped her shoulders, shaking her a little. "How many times has Lord Leigh kissed you, Isla? And you never thought to tell me?"

"I did not want you to think badly of me. You know what I feel about him."

"Well, are you sure you do not feel more for him other than annoyance? Kissing the man tells me that you like him and that perhaps your anger at his lordship stems from jealousy."

Isla gaped at her friend, pulling out of her hold to start pacing once more. "Of course, it does not." And yet, a little niggling tidbit of doubt crept into her voice. She had liked Lord Leigh before overhearing his conversation with his friends. She had hoped that maybe there may be a friendship that would grow into more. But his cold, calculated words toward marrying a woman with money soon changed all that. No, she was no longer jealous. Of course she was not.

"I think we need to leave the house party. I cannot keep running into him, for when I do, I forget all my scruples and principles and keep allowing the rogue to kiss me. Which, I might add," she said, holding up a finger, "he does very well, but that is beside the point. We ought to go home, prepare for the Season and leave all these title-chasing and inheritance-hunting aristocrats to their own devices."

"We only have a week left, Isla. I'm certain we can stay, and you can keep your distance from Lord Leigh. If you want to, of course," her friend suggested, a teasing note in her tone.

Isla gaped, unsure she had heard Harlow correctly. "You think I cannot keep away from him? Of course, I can," she declared, certain she could and would do as she stated. She would not let the lure of Lord Leigh's kisses get to her again and make her resolve to hate him for all eternity ease.

"Very good then," Harlow said, starting for the door. "So let us go downstairs. I've come to collect you as we're having a picnic down by the lake today. The servants are setting up the tables and food as we speak."

Isla took a deep, calming breath, reaching for her bonnet and stepping before the looking glass to check that her gown was in order. Her light-blue muslin dress was pretty and perhaps not as fancy as the other ladies present, but she did not care about that. They were not raised to care about the materialistic things in life, how large their dowries were, none of that had ever mattered, and she wasn't about to wear silks and diamonds and all but announce to rogues like Lord Leigh that she too was an heiress.

They made their way into the drawing room and found that the party was already outdoors and moving toward the lake. Isla and Harlow followed at a relaxed pace. She pulled her bonnet on, tying the blue ribbons about her chin, and studied the group ahead of them.

Lord Kempt and Lady Hirch, the Earl of Hirch's widow, were walking separate from the others, and Isla wondered if they had been the couple she had heard last night before being accosted by Lord Leigh.

The thought of his lordship, of being stuck in the closet with him, his eager lips and fingers that did delicious, wicked things to her bombarded her mind. Heat kissed her entire body, and she fanned her face as they made it to the tables covered with white linen and the finest china for their picnic.

She sat and adjusted her seat, settling her skirts about her legs, and looked up and met the heavy-lidded, hungry gaze of Lord Leigh several paces away. Her stomach twisted and flipped, her breathing hitched. Somehow with just a glance, she knew what he was thinking, what he was remembering, and if she was so bold to assume, what he wanted to do again if the ravenous look in his eye was any indication.

"Oh dear," Harlow said at her side, clearing her throat.

Isla tore her gaze away from Lord Leigh to her friend. "What is wrong?" she asked her.

Harlow chuckled, sipping a glass of lemonade. "I fear that your determination to keep away from Lord Leigh will be disputed by the lordship himself. He seems quite fixated on you if I'm any judge of character."

A pleasant warmness flowed through her blood at her friend's words before she thrust the reaction aside. What was she doing! She did not like the man or what he stood for. She had to be strong in her judgment of him. How dare he marry women under false pretenses, even if he promised to keep them well pleased. She doubted they would be well pleased when he fornicated outside of the marriage bed and gave them the pox.

"I shall ignore the man, just as I promised to do. His kisses have no effect on me whatsoever," she said, shifting her attention to the other tables. "Have you noticed that no one has sat with us?" Isla remarked. "That is very odd, is it not? Have we done something to offend the other ladies, do you think? I thought we were becoming close friends."

"Maybe," Harlow said, a mischievous light in her eyes. "They have noticed Lord Leigh's preoccupation with you and do not welcome it."

That was the last thing Isla wanted. She wanted only to help the ladies keep well clear of men such as Lord Leigh. But mayhap, his lordship was right. Maybe the ladies present did not care that he was seeking a fortune, as they were indeed seeking a title.

Her sheltered life at Grafton had not allowed her to see much workings of the *ton*, but she had heard it was fickle and cruel at times. Were all the rumors true? Were the women just as scandalous and malevolent as the men?

Lord Billington called out to anyone who wished to fish, and Harlow almost tipped over her chair in her haste to stand. "Oh, I must try fishing. I have never been before," she said, smiling from ear to ear as she started toward his lordship. Isla noted she was the only woman at the picnic who did.

Out of her peripheral vision, she noticed Lord Leigh excuse himself from his conversation and start toward her. She steeled herself to be cold and unaffected by his presence. An unlikely aspiration when her body went against her wishes and all but swooned with the notion of him being near her.

Damn it all to hell. How was she ever to maintain her distance from the man?

She kept watching Harlow as she took the fishing rod from Lord Billington, an eager student as he explained the parts. Lord Leigh sat beside her, shuffling his chair closer to hers. She cast him a displeased glance, and his knowing grin made her want to bare her teeth at him or kiss him merely to wipe that obnoxious look off his face.

"Pleased to see me, Isla?" he asked her, one brow raised in question. "Your blue gown is very fetching but not as nice as your shift. I think I shall forever hold a soft spot for your unmentionables."

"You cad," she whispered furiously. "Do you have any scruples?"

He scoffed. "Not really. Not when I'm around you, at least. You make me want to do bad things."

She swallowed, lifting her chin, refusing to melt into a pool of desire at his feet. That's what he wanted, of course, or to send her fleeing to the house like some green debutante. Which, of course, she was. Not that she could claim such a title anymore. Not with Lord Leigh cornering her in cupboards and tempting her to do things no lady of class ever would do.

Lady Susan sauntered over to them, sitting at their table. She smiled at Isla, but something about the lady's

TAMARA GILL

eyes put her on guard. Maybe the ladies were angry with her? And she knew exactly who to blame. The lump of delicious, annoying flesh beside her.

"Lord Leigh, Miss Woodville, is there room for one more at your table?" she asked sweetly, giving his lordship a coquettish glance.

Lord Leigh leaned forward, reaching for the jug of lemonade before pouring Lady Susan a glass and refilling Isla's. "Of course, Lady Susan. The more, the merrier," he answered. A sweet gesture, all told, but the feeling of his hand against her leg pulled her from her more considerate thoughts toward the man.

She met his gaze, a warning light in his eyes telling her to not say a word along with the banked-up need she had often caught him watching her with. Her stomach twisted into knots at the feel of his touch. She reached for her drink, downing a good portion of it before reaching down and pushing his hand away to no avail.

He pouted, and she shook her head, not quite believing he would try such a scandalous thing right before Lady Susan.

"Thirsty, Miss Woodville?" Lady Susan said, her tinkling laugh a pitch too high to be genuine. "But then you have been busy at this house party. Enough so that anyone would be parched with thirst, I would think."

Lord Leigh's hand stilled on her leg, and the look he threw Lady Susan was ice.

"The house party has been eventful and full of activities. Lord Billington could certainly not be accused of hosting a dreary party, that is for sure," she answered, not rising to Lady Susan's bait if it was indeed intended to be so.

"Absolutely," Lady Susan stated, her tone reeking of

86

distaste. "Although I did think there would be an announcement or two of understandings between the guests. To have none at all is a little surprising."

"Really?" Lord Leigh queried. "I have been to many house parties, and no betrothal has been announced. I do not find that there is anything to be concerned about."

"Of course, Lord Leigh. You have been most attentive to all of us ladies, which we're very fond of, as you well know." The look that Lady Susan gave Lord Leigh was anything but innocent. It looked predatory.

She clamped her mouth shut, annoyance running through her at the thought of Lady Susan trying her wiles on Lord Leigh. A distressing thought indeed, for Isla could not say with absolute certainty that it was because he was a fortune hunter, and she wanted her to be safe from such vultures. Or if the thought of Lord Leigh kissing anyone the way he had kissed her left a hollow pit in her stomach.

The realization struck her, and she stood. Her chair toppled backward, and she glanced at both Lord Leigh and Lady Susan. They watched her, Lady Susan with smug satisfaction. Lord Leigh, however, appeared concerned at her distressed countenance. "If you would excuse me. I need to return to the house."

Isla fled, not caring what anyone thought. She just knew she had to get away from Lord Leigh and the jealousy that spiked through her blood, leaving it hot and angry at anyone who wanted him for themselves.

Anyone who was not her.

TWELVE

Duke excused himself from Lady Susan, ignoring the startled, mumbled communication that spilled forth from her pinched lips at his leaving, and went after Isla. Something had distressed her, and he was certain it had not been his hand. Even though touching her had been all he thought of from the moment she left him in the closet the night before.

He had taken himself in hand back in his room. The thought of her stretched out on his bed, her long, brown locks strewn over his pillow, had been all that it took to come.

Even now, she was all he thought of. Not merely to tease, which he enjoyed immensely, but to simply be in her company. She was a steadying presence, kind and welcoming to all. So different to the other ladies at the ball whom he knew wanted him for his title as much as he needed them for their money.

No matter whom he chose, the union would not be the happiest of marriages. Even so, the worrying thoughts of his impending marriage were the least of his concerns. Not

ON A WILD DUKE CHASE

when Isla had looked genuinely upset. She had paled and panicked before his eyes, but why?

He increased his pace, thinking back to what Lady Susan had said. She had complimented him on his attention and care toward the ladies at the house party before throwing him a look that he'd seen often on the finest courtesans in London. A look that told him he could tumble her in any closet or room in the grand house behind them anytime he wanted, and she would not complain.

Isla had seen that look, and it distressed her.

He checked her whereabouts and saw her enter through the library. A room that had been off-limits to the guests. He went via the terrace and parlor, not wanting to raise suspicion, but used an interior door to enter Lord Billington's library.

He caught Isla pacing before the unlit hearth. She halted at his interruption and did not say a word, merely watched him. Her color was high, bright, rosy cheeks that made her appear flushed and bothered.

"I was right, was I not?" he asked, taking his time coming closer. Her eyes were wide as if she could take flight at any moment. He did not want to scare her away. He wanted her to never leave if he were being honest.

"About what?" she asked, taking a deep breath that pushed her ample bosom up in her gown. He bit back a groan, his obsession with the chit beyond the pale.

"Outside just now with Lady Susan. Her words regarding my attention to the ladies caused you distress, not entirely because of what she said, but how she looked at me. You saw that look, did you not? And you did not like it."

Her lips pursed, and she narrowed her eyes. Hell, she was beautiful. So wonderfully obstinate and different from everyone else. How could he not follow her back to the house? How could he not follow her anywhere?

"I do not care what you do with Lady Susan. It is your life. I have no say in it."

"Liar," he accused, towering over her, her small gasp making her lips part in the most mind-altering way. "Admit you like me despite your hatred for my plans for a wife."

She threw up her hands, gesturing wildly. "Fine, I shall admit it. I think you are too handsome for your own good and I think you know it. I thought you the most kind and sweet gentleman upon meeting you at this house party, but my opinion of you changed the moment I heard your discussion in the library with your friends."

He nodded. Finally, he knew why she had been determined to cause an issue with him and the other ladies he had been trying to court. Not that he could concentrate on any of them. Not with this chit always about and distracting him.

Even now, he wanted to dismiss their argument and pull her into his arms and kiss away her denial. She would relent. She would kiss him back. He knew it as well as he knew he would take another breath.

"Men marry for money all the time, and women marry for rank and prestige. I regret you overheard a short, callous conversation, but you have not been in society, Isla. You will learn next year at your Season just how cutthroat the *ton* can be in getting their own way."

"I will not marry for money or prestige. I want to marry for love. How can anything last, withstand life's trials if it is not based on friendship and affection? I feel sorry for you, Lord Leigh. You will rue the day you marry for convenience. And I hope this conversation comes back and haunts you as a time where you could have chosen differently when you did not."

He swallowed, the pit of his stomach churning at her words. He did not want a marriage of convenience. Each time he was around Isla, he understood that more and more. But what was he to do? How could he seek the woman before him when she did not come with any money to save his name? To save his mother from the lie she was punished for?

"You speak as if you will have a choice on your future, but you will not. Do you have a substantial dowry, Isla? Are you an heiress, and no one knows? If you do not, your mama, like all the others, will push you toward men like me, and you will marry one of us. Do not crow so soon that you have better morals than I."

She glanced away, swallowing, and he narrowed his eyes on her. "Are you an heiress?" he asked again. He didn't want to hope that she was, for then he could marry a woman whom he liked and enjoyed her company, no matter their bickering, and she could save him too. She would not believe him, of course, but he could make her believe him in time.

"I am not an heiress," she said, clearing her throat. "Do not pretend that admission disappoints you, Lord Leigh."

"No matter what you believe, I do not go around kissing women at house parties. I have only kissed you, and I only want to kiss you." And he could not have her. She would never be his. The pain that shot through his chest made him catch his breath, and he moved over to the settee, sitting.

He glanced up and found her watching him. What was she thinking? Did she feel the same? Did she want him as much as he wanted her?

"Please kiss me one more time, and I promise to leave you to find the grand love of your life." The man who would not be him.

How he hated his father right at that moment. For squandering the family fortune, leaving the bare minimum to run the estates. Leaving his mother to rot in Bedlam for crimes she did not commit.

She worked her clasped hands before her, and he could see she was debating his request. He had never begged a woman before for their touch, and yet, if she did not come to him, he was certain he would die from her denial of him.

He saw the moment she decided, and gasped as she threw herself onto his lap, her lips taking his in a kiss that sent him reeling. He clutched at her, holding her steadfast lest she fled from him forever.

Her tongue tangled with his, their breaths mingled. He moaned as her hand moved beneath his coat, sliding along his waistcoat and shirt. Her touch left fire in its wake. No matter their differences, their many arguments, they knew how to do well together in this way. He was utterly in lust with her and never wanted her to leave him.

Lust, Duke? Are you sure it is only that? his mind taunted.

He ignored his thoughts, reveling in the feel of her on his lap. Her ample bosom constrained against his chest, her soft, round bottom pressing against his growing cock. She seemed to understand what she was doing to him and wiggled, sending fire to course through his blood.

"I should not be doing this," she breathed, breaking the kiss. "But you are right. I cannot get enough of you either, as furious and distracted as you make me."

Her words sent relief to pour through him, and he took her mouth in a punishing kiss. He wanted her to remember this. He wanted her to always think of him when she kissed another man.

His hands were everywhere, mentally imprinting her on his mind to get him through the many years ahead.

Marry her. Find another way to make up the money your father lost. Sell the London town house.

"Enough," she said, moving from his lap. He reached for her, wanting her back in his arms, but she shook her head. "No, Lord Leigh. No more." A pained expression flittered across her face before she blinked, and it was gone. "Marry your heiress, and make the best of your marriage. I do wish you well."

She left the room, and he heard her order the footman to fetch her maid. She would leave the house party. He knew it to his very bones. Duke stared at the unlit hearth, fire and pain coursing through his blood in equal parts. He leaned on his knees, steepling his hands. He would not go after her. He could not, even though his body roared to do exactly that.

He had to let her go. He had to save his mother and keep all those employed at his estates engaged. There was no other choice, even if he wished for such a different future right now.

A future with Isla Woodville, as poor as they would be.

CHAPTER

THIRTEEN

The Season 1806

Isla made her curtsy to Queen Charlotte and was now officially out in society and ready to commence her first Season. Her mama had outdone herself, hiring the finest modiste in London and having her dressed to perfection like those who ruled London during the social swirl. Her gowns were of the finest silk, and a maid was hired just to prepare her hair each evening for the events she attended.

Her sister Hailey, now the Duchess of Derby, was back in London, having come home from their honeymoon abroad to support her in her first foray into the *haute ton*.

The balls and dinners so far were beyond what Isla had imagined, and thankfully her friend Harlow had accompanied her in town, her family taking up residence not far from where they stayed on Grosvenor Square.

She was glad of her company, for Harlow was the only person who knew what she suffered. A broken heart from a man who, in truth, did not deserve to hold her love at all in his power. But he did.

She took a deep, calming breath and made her thanks and felicitations to Lord and Lady Collins, who were hosting tonight's ball.

The ballroom, upon entering, was a feast for one's eyes. Several crystal chandeliers glowed above the polished ballroom floor, reflecting off the wooden surfaces and the glittering gold leaf on the furniture. Her ladyship had infused the room with bouquets of roses, and the sweet scent went some way in stunting the nauseating smells of cologne and sweat.

They moved through the throng of guests, greeting those who they knew as they went to find a place in which to stand and enjoy the night's revelry. Isla spotted several gentlemen who had taken a keen interest in her, and she smiled in welcome, but the gesture went only skin deep.

None of the men sparked anything deeper within her. None challenged her or disagreed with her. None of them, in turn, made her stomach flutter and her heart race. Whatever would she do if she did not find a gentleman who gave her a little of what she felt with Lord Leigh?

"Isla, do not look, but Lord Leigh is here. He's leading Lady Susan out onto the dance floor." Her friend Harlow nodded in the direction but did not look directly.

Isla was not so subtle. She glanced to where Harlow suggested and met the startled gaze of Lord Leigh. His steps faltered before he righted his footing and proceeded to ready himself with his dance with Lady Susan.

The Marquess of Craig's daughter looked well pleased and smug in Lord Leigh's arms. And so she should be, Isla supposed. She would gain a viscountess title, and he would gain her fortune. What a triumph marriage for them both.

She could not tear her eyes from him. He had not changed in the few months since she had seen him last. The day she had kissed him in Lord Billington's library had been the day she fled back to Grafton. She knew if she remained at the York estate, she would crumble, make an error of judgment that she could not take back.

She would have lain with him, and he would not have married her since he believed her to be of meager funds. Her parents had married for love, and now so too her sister. She was determined to do the same. The heroines in her books always gained their happy ever after, and there was a man out there for her. She was sure of it. A man who would love her and make her feel all she had felt with Lord Leigh. She merely had to find him.

Isla sighed. To think Lord Leigh was that person was an error she needed to forget. He required an heiress to keep himself out of debtor's prison. Isla wanted a love match. Their paths, therefore, had no reason to cross again.

His dance with Lady Susan seemed pleasant, and Lady Susan laughed and fluttered her lashes at his lordship at every opportunity. That he did not look in her direction again told Isla everything she needed to know. He had moved on, forgotten about her, and that was for the best. She would not marry him merely to save his financial woes. She deserved better than that.

"I know you do not like to talk about it, but are you well, Isla? You do look a little out of sorts."

Isla threw her friend a consoling smile. "I am fine, Harlow. It is merely a shock to see him again after so long."

"Did he write to you at all?" Harlow asked.

Isla accepted a glass of ratafia from a passing footman and took a fortifying sip, needing to remove the lump wedged in her throat. "No. Not once, not even to apologize." Not that he needed to say sorry for anything. Not really. He was honest with her and told her of his needs. If anything, she was the one who had lied. She had told him she was not as wealthy as she was. As wealthy as all of her sisters were. If he married Lady Susan and found out about her lie after the fact, she wondered if he would be angry. If he would seek her out and demand to know why she had said what she did.

That she was not an heiress when she was.

And she would have to tell him it was because she wanted him to love her for the little he thought she did have, not for what she actually could give him. How could she give herself to someone for something as invaluable as money?

She could not.

"Are you going to be well enough to see out the Season with his lordship in town? You may witness many such nights with him paying court to someone else. I do not want your Season to be ruined or upsetting to you," her friend said, reaching out and placing a comforting hand on her arm.

Isla shook her head, determined to move forward. She could not change Lord Leigh's determination to marry money. But she could determine who gained access to hers. A man who loved her. That was what she wanted.

But you will lose him...

The thought haunted her, and her gaze stubbornly slipped back to Lord Leigh and Lady Susan. They made a striking pair. They were a beautiful couple. For he was titled, and she was rich. She had never been one for petty feelings or hating anyone for any reason that was not warranted, but she disliked Lady Susan at that very moment. Not because she wished to marry to gain a title, but because it would mean she would lose Lord Leigh.

She schooled her features, blinking back the tears that horrifyingly filled her eyes. She would not cry. Not here and not before the *ton*.

The dance came to an end, and Lady Susan clutched at Lord Leigh as if he were some lifeline she had to hold on to to remain in this glittering world.

He escorted her off the ballroom floor, his gaze moving back to her just before she lost them in the crowd. "If you'll excuse me, Harlow. I need the use of the retiring room." She fled the room, needing air, space, a quiet place to think.

She made her way upstairs to where a maid directed her and moved along the hall. This part of the house was quieter than she presumed it to be. The muffled sounds of the ball floated through the house, along with the sound of her slippered feet on the Aubusson rug.

"Isla!"

The familiar voice sent a shiver down her spine. She increased her steps, slipping into the retiring room only to find it empty. The door opened behind her, and she stumbled out of the way as Lord Leigh burst into the room, shutting and locking the door behind him.

"What are you doing?" she accused him. "You cannot be in here. We'll be caught, and then your plan to marry Lady Susan will be thwarted."

"I did not know you were in London," he said.

That was all he had to say? He did not know she was in town? "We arrived three weeks ago and have been renting a house in Grosvenor Square. I have made my curtsy to the queen and have attended several events. I'm not hiding my presence here in town if that is what you're wondering."

"And have you found any gentlemen to your liking?" he

asked, his dark, hooded eyes flashing with something she could not discern.

She shook her head. "Not yet, but it's early in the Season. I'm certain I shall, not that I need to tell you anything about it." She wanted to hurt him, say mean things even if they only served to make her feel better. After seeing him with Lady Susan this evening, she could not pull forth an ounce of pleasantness toward his lordship. The sight of him with another lady hurt too much.

"I, too, have been having a very successful time in town. Without the interruptions from a certain lady, whenever I speak to women. It makes courting much easier, I find."

"You're an arse. Has anyone ever told you that?" she asked him, and by the look of his shocked expression, no one ever had.

"You have bite, Miss Woodville. I would not have thought it possible from you," he said, his tone one of sarcasm.

They stared at each other, and Isla did not know what to say or do next. Emotions boiled up within her, and she bit her tongue, trying to stop the tears that returned. Damn the man for getting under her skin. For making her feel things for him he did not deserve.

His smug expression vanished, and before she knew what he was about, she was in his arms, his strong, immovable embrace engulfing her. For a moment, she did not know what she ought to do, but her body overrode her startled mind, and she clutched at him, holding him with as much force as he held her.

"I'm sorry," he whispered into her hair, kissing her temple. "I'm sorry. I did not want to upset you. I did not follow you to upset you. I merely wanted to see you. To know that you have not promised yourself to anyone. I could not stand that."

She sniffed, the scent of his cologne making her mind befuddled. "What does it matter if I have? The talk about town is that you're going to marry Lady Susan."

He frowned down at Isla. He drew back a little and pushed several strands of her hair away from her face. "If I could marry you, Isla, I would. You must know that, no matter how curt I have been toward you, it is not because I do not care. It is because I care too much. I want something that I cannot have. I want you to have more than I can give you."

"Just ask me. I promise everything will be well," she begged of him. Needing him to ask her now, before he didn't, and everything was ruined.

"There is more to my life, that you...that no one knows. Things that may change your opinion of me. You would not marry me even if you had the choice, not if you knew..."

He stepped out of her hold, and she reached for him, halting him. "What secret? I know that you require funds to marry. What more is there to know?" she begged him, beseeching him to tell her.

He cradled her face in his hands, staring down at her. "You deserve better than what I can give you, Isla. And if we married, the burden of my life would be heavy. I do not want that for you."

"But what about what I want?" she stated, clasping the lapels of his coat. "I want you. Let me love you." She had to be enough for him as he thought of her now. A woman with a modest dowry, not an heiress. If he chose her now, she could save him, and no matter what other secrets he harbored, she knew she could shoulder those.

"There are too many who rely on me, Isla. I cannot be

selfish to choose myself and my happiness over all who look to me for leadership and security."

Disappointment ran through her blood like poison. He may want her as much as she wanted him, but it was not enough to outweigh his need for financial security. She was not enough.

"Then you best marry Lady Susan and secure your future, Lord Leigh. I hope it is a happy union." She walked to the door, opened it, and gasped.

Lady Collins, Lady Francesca, and Miss Jones stood on the threshold, their mouths agape, their eyes wide. Their attention slipped past Isla and landed on Lord Leigh, their eyes growing wider with alarm.

Lady Collins pushed past Isla, a short, stubby finger lifting and pointing at each of them. "Are you in the retiring room with Lord Leigh unchaperoned, Miss Woodville?" her ladyship asked, but it was more like a statement of fact.

Isla felt the blood drain from her face. This was not what she wanted at all. She wanted a marriage of love and affection. Not one brought on with scandal and ruination. The sound of retreating slippered feet caught her attention, and she looked back to the door and noticed Lady Francesca had disappeared.

Panic assailed her, and she clasped Lady Collins's hand. "Nothing untoward occurred, your ladyship. I became lost, and Lord Leigh was in this room when I entered it, looking for the retiring room. You happened upon us just before I was about to leave."

"Really?" her ladyship said, a disbelieving brow raised. "You are telling me, Miss Woodville, that Lord Leigh was using the lady's retiring room as a place to rest during my ball?" Her ladyship turned to Lord Leigh. "Might I ask why you were in the lady's retiring room, my lord?"

A muscle worked at Lord Leigh's jaw, and Isla could see the disappointment, the regret and pain that crossed his features at being caught with her. He truly had not wished to marry her at all. She had hoped he could have looked beyond his need for money, but it would seem he could not. His financial woes overrode all his other wants and needs, and now, being caught with her alone, that future he hoped for was fading away.

"I sought out Miss Woodville as I wanted to ask her to be my wife, and she has agreed. We wanted to surprise everyone with a notice in *The Times*, but it would seem you have thwarted my plans." He walked up to Isla and picked up her gloved hand, kissing it. "Wish us well, Lady Collins. You are the first to know our news."

Her ladyship's countenance changed, and turning to Miss Jones, who stood at the door, mouth still agape, clapped her hands. "Oh, wonderful news! We shall announce your happy news now, come, we shall return to the ball together, so all will know nothing scandalous was afoot." Her ladyship bustled out of the room, and Isla looked up at Lord Leigh, but he refused to look at her. The smile he had just forced before Lady Collins was wiped from his face as they followed one of the matrons of the *ton* back downstairs.

Isla's head swam, hopes and dreams dissipated. This was not how she wanted her marriage proposal to have gone. And this was certainly not how she wanted her future husband to react to marrying her.

What a mitigated disaster her Season had turned into. Some would say a triumph, an unknown miss from Northamptonshire had secured Viscount Leigh, but she was not one of them. And nor was his lordship.

CHAPTER

FOURTEEN

The remainder of the night was a blur of congratulations, toasts, and talk of his future bride and their wedding. Questions bombarded him as to when they would marry, how long they had been courting. Had their affection for each other grown while at Lord Billington's house party.

He stood beside Isla, noting her quiet and modest countenance. She looked as shocked as he was at the turn of events, and he only had himself to blame. He should not have gone after her, not followed her into that retiring room.

Idiot fool. What had he been thinking!

"I shall write to Mr. Woodville tonight and send word for him to come to town. He will want to meet you, Lord Leigh, and you may discuss the marriage contracts then," Mrs. Woodville said to him, smiling down at her daughter, seemingly oblivious to her child's pale, wan visage.

"So soon, Mama?" Isla said, her voice tired. "Surely, there is no need to rush these things. In some cases, the marriage between two people does not occur for several months, or even years."

Isla's mother looked at her, confused. "But that is not the case with you, my darling. The union between you and Lord Leigh may progress at a normal pace. We shall have the first banns called this Sunday and for the next three Sundays following."

A month. He had a month to speak with his steward and see where they could make up some money. Try to drag his pitiful coffers into something that would give him more than what he had now to live on. With a wife with little dowry, it merely added another mouth to feed. He was unsure how he could afford a wedding and now keep his new bride in the station in which she was accustomed.

She would soon see the state of his Hampshire Estate. The many paintings, furniture, rugs, and curtains that had been sold after his father's death in trying to keep people employed. As it was, he had to let go half his staff, and the house and grounds suffered for it.

A good marriage was what he had needed. He fought the panic that assailed him. How was he to bring his mother home? Pay to have her removed from Bedlam, an institution into which she should never have been placed?

She would now die there. Alone and believing she was unloved.

What had he done?

"Send word to my house at St. James Square when Mr. Woodville is in town, and I shall call on him then." He bowed before Isla, unable to quite meet her eye. "Good evening, my dear. I shall see you then as well." Duke turned on his heel and left, not bothering to stop and talk to anyone on his way out. He needed to go, think, and plan.

He could not do any of that in the middle of a ball.

He was sunk, and his new, poor wife would join him in that ruination.

Duke cringed at the disrespectful thought. It was not Isla's fault he had lost all his money. Nor was it his, but his father's. Even so, she had not asked him to follow her into that room. She had not asked anything from him except to let her love him, and even then, he had thrown her wishes back at her.

She deserved so much better than what he could give her or what he was.

Fool.

A week later, he received a missive from Mr. Woodville requesting an audience with him that afternoon to discuss the marriage contracts and particulars of the wedding. Duke leaned back on his chair behind his desk, throwing the missive on the mahogany table before him, one of the pieces of furniture he had not been able to part with, no matter how much money it would fetch.

He sat there for a time, hoping that Isla may have at least five thousand pounds to her name. That would help, not indefinitely, but a little was better than none. He rubbed a hand over his jaw and sighed. Sitting here accomplished nothing, and better he found out now what his financial situation would be rather than after he married her.

It did not take him long to get to Woodville's home, a larger Georgian mansion he had not thought would be affordable for such a humble family. The duke, he remembered. Derby most likely put them up in such comforts now that he was part of their family. But then Isla had mentioned the Woodville's leasing it, so mayhap he was wrong.

He knocked on the door, and it was promptly answered by a young footman. "Lord Leigh, you are expected. Please come in," the young man said. "May I take your coat, my lord?"

Leigh waved the offer aside. "No, thank you."

The young man gestured toward a room near the front of the house. "This way if you please."

Duke followed him and entered the library, much better stocked than his own. An older gentleman, well dressed and with graying hair, stood, calling him to enter. "Lord Leigh, how good it is to meet you." The man came about the desk and shook his hand, offering him a chair. "Come, sit. We have much to discuss."

He smiled at the man, a jovial fellow it would seem, and wondered just how much he needed to talk about. "Thank you for meeting with me, Mr. Woodville. I know this betrothal is very untoward. I should have asked for your permission first, but then..."

"Never mind that, Lord Leigh. I know that these things happen with more spontaneity than normal when the heart wants what it wants." Mr. Woodville smiled at him as if he expected him to agree.

"Of course," he said, not wanting to give offense. He was a right bastard. Here was Isla's father, excited and happy for his daughter's forthcoming marriage, and all Duke could think about was what she would cost him in gowns and shoes each month. However would he afford to keep a wife happy?

"Now, may I call you Leigh? I find adding honorifics in private to be tiring."

"Of course," he said again, making a mental note to answer with something other than *of course* when asked another question.

"I thought we ought to go over the marriage contracts first. Get that side of the business out of the way, and then we shall retire for luncheon. I know my wife is particularly excited to welcome you officially to our family, and you shall meet another of our daughters. Miss Julia has come up to town with me, but of course, she is not out as yet."

"Of—" Duke stopped himself from answering the same yet again. "Lunch sounds wonderful." He shifted his chair closer to the desk. "Shall we proceed?" he asked Mr. Woodville.

"Yes, yes, of course." The older man opened a drawer on his desk, pulling out several papers. "Now, before we begin, I would like you to know and understand that what I'm about to tell you must stay between us. You may discuss this now with the Duke of Derby, for he has married our darling Hailey, but as part of the family, this secret is guarded and for reasons that you will soon come to understand."

Duke gaped at Mr. Woodville. Oh dear God, there was some family secret that she too hid? His mind worked furiously, thinking of what it could be. He did not need another tribulation to pile upon him.

"What is it, Mr. Woodville?" he asked.

"Please, call me Edward." The older man shuffled through his papers, sliding several over to him. "This is the usual contract information between uniting our two families, the date of the wedding and who will officiate the ceremony, location, etcetera."

Duke read through the document, seeing all that Mr. Woodville—Edward—had just mentioned written in black ink. He turned to the next page, the name of her childhood home listed as an asset upon the death of her parents. To be sold and income passed on in equal values to each daughter. His eyes skimmed over the figure of her dowry before he went back to it. "There is an error in the document, sir," he said, pointing to the sum.

Mr. Woodville leaned over the desk, staring down to where Duke's finger sat. "No, no, that is correct."

Duke swallowed the bile that rose in his throat. "Excuse me, Mr. Woodville. But that cannot be right." He read the sum again, counting the number of naughts in the sum. "Miss Woodville cannot be worth such a sum." His stomach revolted at the amount, and he swallowed, sure he was about to cast up his accounts.

Mr. Woodville chuckled. "Oh, she's not worth that measly sum. She is priceless, but to you and your future, that is what my darling Isla brings with her." Mr. Woodville frowned, clearly sensing Duke's distress. "Did you not know she is an heiress, Lord Leigh?"

Duke stared at his soon-to-be father-in-law, unable to form words. She was rich? An heiress. His stomach recoiled at the way he had stayed away from her this past week since their announcement at Lady Collin's ball. He had been sick with worry, and yet, all the time, she was worth more than many of the women he had been seeking to court.

"I did not know," he said, his voice hoarse. He felt as if he would vomit, and he knew the reason why. She had told him herself. Just ask me, and all will be well. And he had not trusted her. He had not loved her enough to let go of his need for funds to marry her. And she knew that truth as well as he did.

She would hate him as much as he hated himself for not seeing past his need for money to what he truly wanted.

Her.

CHAPTER
FIFTEEN

"Well, that is good news for me, then, for then I know that you are not a fortune-hunting good-for-nothing whom I would have to call out for being caught alone in a retiring room with my daughter."

The steel in Mr. Woodville's tone brought Duke's gaze up to meet his, and he heard the warning in the man's voice and knew he was being chastised for his slip of etiquette.

"I apologize for that, Mr. Woodville. I should not have followed Isla to that room, but I wished to ask for her hand," he lied, unable to tell her father the truth, for he would indeed then boot him out of the house and refuse to allow her to marry him after all. Ruination and scandal bedamned.

Something told Duke that Mr. Woodville, for all his friendliness, was not a man to cross. Not when it came to his daughters.

"What you now know of my daughters' dowries must remain confidential. If the *ton* found out that they were worth such a sum, they would be hounded from dawn to

110

dusk during their Seasons. We may not be titled, but we are not without means. The gentlemen whom my daughters choose to be their husbands will love them for who they are, not what they will bring to the marriage."

"I understand," he said, guilt crushing him from within. "Should we sign the contract and have some luncheon?" Duke suggested.

Mr. Woodville smiled, dipping a quill and handing it to him. "Sign away, Lord Leigh, and let us be done with work."

Duke signed his name and watched as Mr. Woodville did the same before ringing for a servant. He rolled up the document and sealed it closed with wax. "Have this sent directly to my solicitor on Warwick Lane, just off Newgate Street. Have Thomas take it and ensure it is placed in Mr. Lipton's hand himself."

The older servant nodded. "I will send Thomas posthaste, Mr. Woodville."

Isla's father leaned back in his chair, smiling. "Now, shall we have lunch? I do not know about you, Leigh, but I'm hungry and our cook does the best roasted potatoes, and we have beef for lunch. It should be delicious indeed."

Duke's stomach grumbled. It had been several days since he had eaten anything remotely satisfying. Cheese and bread could only sustain someone for so long. The thought of vegetables, gravy, and meat made his mouth water.

They made their way into the dining room, and he found Mrs. Woodville already seated, along with a young lady whom he had never met before, but there was no mistaking her for Isla's sister.

He bowed before them. "Good afternoon. Thank you for having me for lunch, Mrs. Woodville," he said.

She smiled, gesturing for him to sit across from her.

"The pleasure is ours, Lord Leigh." She looked toward the door. "Isla will not be long, I'm certain."

Duke nodded, but he knew why she was avoiding him, for the same reasons he had been avoiding her this past week. She knew his secret. That he was indeed a fortune hunter who had fooled Mr. Woodville into thinking it was a love match. That his daughter was marrying a man she loved, not one who had made a mistake that just happened to turn out to his advantage.

The sound of slippered feet on the foyer floor caught his attention, and he looked toward the dining room door just as Isla entered the room. She did not look at him, merely dipped into a curtsy to her parents and sat beside him. He could feel the tension that radiated off her in waves. She was angry, seething if he were right, and that anger was directed solely toward him.

"You make a handsome pair. After lunch a drive about the park I think would be nice for you both. What do you think, my lord?" Mrs. Woodville asked of him, nodding to the butler to commence service.

"I think that would be lovely indeed," Mr. Woodville agreed with his wife before he could answer.

Duke looked at Isla and hoped her parents did not notice that their daughter was less than pleased at being seated beside him or having to go out on a carriage ride. They had started as friends, and although by his own stupid actions they were now betrothed, he would win her friendship and mayhap more in the weeks to come. He had asked for her hand to save her reputation, with a large dowry or not. That had to count for something.

"I have a headache, Mama. I do not feel like a carriage ride today," she said, thanking a servant who placed down the first course of turtle soup.

"I will send a parasol with you, my dear, and have a tisane made up before you leave, but you really ought to be seen together. It has been a week, and neither of you has been seen in society since Lord and Lady Collins' ball. We do not want anyone to think anything is amiss, do we?" Isla's mother stated, pinning him with a look that brooked no argument.

Duke nodded, not willing to go against anything Isla's parents said. The remainder of the lunch passed in reasonable benign conversation. Isla continued to give one-word answers, even when her parents queried this or that regarding the wedding.

Their afternoon carriage ride would not be pleasant, he feared.

A little after lunch, he helped Isla up into her family carriage, following close on her heels. She sat as far away from him as she could on the seat, a mulish look on her face. "You will have to speak to me at some point, Isla. We're to be married after all."

"Yes, do not remind me of the fact that the very man I'm marrying is one I do not love and who does not love me in return. But I would think he is quite pleased with the turn of events now that he knows that I'm an heiress."

The carriage rolled forward along the square, and he sighed, unsure himself how to go about fixing all that was wrong between them. "I'm sorry this is not what you wanted, and I should not have followed you into the retiring room. I compromised you and had no choice but to offer you my hand in marriage. You must see that."

"I see that very well, but why you followed me, I cannot fathom. You had just finished telling me you could not marry me because I had no dowry. You ought to have left immediately or, better yet, never come into the room at all.

You have stolen my chance at a happy marriage with someone else."

He ground his teeth at the thought of her with anyone else. He leaned close to ensure privacy. "Your kisses tell me that no one else would have sufficed as your husband. You want me as much as I want you, and my following you that night was because I could not bear to see you in pain. Why did you not tell me you were an heiress? Why lie to me about that?"

She twisted on the seat, their noses almost touching. "Oh, what a terrible person I am to want my husband to love me, even a little bit more than he loves my money. Did you find out before Papa told you today of my dowry, or did you follow me that night at the ball because you knew how much I was worth?"

Never in his life had he wanted to strangle a woman as much as he wanted to strangle and, damn it all to hell, kiss the chit before him as he did right now. "I did not know you were an heiress until today."

She scoffed, rolling her eyes. "How fortunate a turn of events for you, Lord Leigh. Now you may save your estates and live life to the fullest, as you obviously have been doing in excess already." She turned to look out the side of the carriage. "No doubt we will soon be as poor as you are now if you spend money enough that you have run out of your inheritance already."

"You are cruel when you want to be," he said, her gasp making her mouth pout in the prettiest manner. "Please keep going past the park," he ordered the driver. "We shall drive around Mayfair instead for a time," he said, not wanting the *ton* to witness their disagreement. "I never lost my inheritance," he continued. "Other than the houses, I inherited nothing but debt. My father is the reason I was left with very little."

"Very little indeed. Only an estate, a London town house, servants, land, and a title. Oh, but I do agree with one point. You were left with very little integrity."

He wanted to tell her of his mother. The real reason he needed a rich bride, but he could not. She would call off the wedding, no matter the scandal, and he could not afford that, for he did need her dowry to save all that he owned. But if Isla found out before the marriage was consummated that his mother was in Bedlam, she would run screaming for the hills.

No family wanted madness to run through their blood even though he was yet to confirm or deny such truth. Not until he met with his mother would he know for certain.

But no one would believe him, even if the secret was to get out now and then a rebuttal. They would assume he would go mad one day just as his mother had presumably done. And any heirs he sired after the fact would befall the same fate.

He needed to have his mother returned, pay to have her erased from Bedlam's files, and have her helped here if she did indeed suffer from disabilities. Try to give her some future that was better than her past. He required Isla for this, but he could not tell her that. One day, but today would not be it.

"I am sorry you are being forced to marry me, and I'm sorry you think that I knew of your financial worth before following you that night, but I did not. I swear on my life, I only knew what your marriage portion will be as of today. I know it is not what you wanted, but please let me try to make a happy life for us both. I do want to be the best husband that I can be. You are, after all, saving everything I hold dear, and I do not want to see you angry and upset."

She crossed her arms over her chest, a muscle working in her jaw.

"There is something between us that is more than anger and differing opinions, and you know there is. We could not keep our hands off each other at the house party, and had we not been interrupted at Lord and Lady Collin's ball, I would have kissed you again. That is a good start, Isla. A good base to build from."

"Lust is not a base for marriage," she said finally.

The word coming from her lips made him inwardly groan. "We were friends first before you overheard my conversation."

"And found out what type of man you really are."

He sat back in the seat, taking a deep breath to calm his ire. The woman was so difficult, he wanted to strangle and kiss her in equal measure. However would he get her to trust him again?

Tell her the truth...

He couldn't just yet, but soon. As soon as they were married, he would tell her. He knew that too was wrong. She could possibly hate him even more for what he would disclose, but it was a risk he had to take. He would not allow her to be ruined due to his error of judgment, and nor could he stand to lose her. He wanted Isla far more than her dowry.

"We have three weeks before the wedding. I shall wear a blue gown. Ensure you're wearing a suit that is complementary to the color."

"We do not need to discuss the wedding yet. I thought we may take this time your parents have granted us for you to ask me any questions about my home in the country or where we shall reside after the wedding."

"You have two homes, is that correct?" she asked him, still not looking at him.

"I do, one in Hampshire and the London town house on St. James Square."

"I would like to see it," she said, meeting his gaze for the first time. "Now, if you please."

Duke hesitated at her request. "I'm not sure that is wise, Isla. We are not married yet."

"Lord Leigh's town house on St. James Square, if you please," she called out to the driver.

He cringed but did not dispute her request. Her anger at him already meant he would not say anything else to displease her. In truth, the thought of her seeing his home, the meager amount of servants, the dust, and empty library shelves and rooms were more alarming than any of the *ton* seeing her enter his abode.

It was shameful but better for her to see just how poor he was now before the wedding and not on their wedding night.

CHAPTER
SIXTEEN

Isla knew she was being particularly cruel to Lord Leigh. Cutting and accusing him at every turn for the wrongs he had done against her. She ought to try to make the marriage one that was at least a little less galling, but she could not.

She was angry at him, and now she wanted to see what her future home looked like. Upon entering the town house, all her hopes that she would walk into a house full of joy and love just as her own had fled. The house was stark, few paintings hung on the walls, family portraits only, no pretty vistas of rural life such as one often sees.

"This is the main foyer." He walked her over to an older gentleman who stooped a little as he stood waiting. "Fordham, this is Miss Isla Woodville, my betrothed, and soon-to-be Viscountess Leigh."

The older man smiled, bowing his head in welcome. "It is lovely to meet you, Miss Woodville."

Isla smiled, pleased to meet him as well. "Thank you, Fordham," she said.

Duke cleared his throat. "I'm going to show Miss

Woodville the town house. You may go about your work, Fordham," his lordship said before the servant hobbled off toward the back of the house.

They walked toward the front of the house and into a library, Isla speculated. The empty bookshelves looked stark and bare, and she wondered how very bad Lord Leigh's financial woes really were. Had he sold everything that was not entailed?

Nothing but stark walls, an unlit, blackened fireplace. Some chairs and a small table covered with dust cloths were left. The only identifying object this was once a library, the desk.

Isla pushed down the pity that rose within her at Lord Leigh's living conditions. His life would change, thanks to her and her money.

"I suppose one of the first things that my funds will have to do is purchase some books for this room. It is a library, is it not?"

He leaned on the desk, his face ashen. "How you must hate me to speak to me in such a way. I am sorry, Isla. I do not know how many times I must tell you how sorry I am."

He would have to tell her many more times before she believed or forgave him. She strolled about the room, closing the library door as she moved past it. "I do not mind buying things for our home, Lord Leigh. In fact, I think I have more than enough dowry to fill many homes over, but I wanted to come here today to give you some rules that I shall not allow to be broken. Even if the moment we marry, I'm no longer in control of my life or the money I bring to the union."

"What are your terms?" he asked, hoping that this may be a step to move past their constant bickering.

"I do not care that the money may be required to pay off

debt accrued by your father or yourself since his death. Repairs of your estates and those of your tenants. I do not mind paying for horses or new vehicles, but I draw the line at paying for your whores or gambling from the day we marry. If you squander my fortune at either of those locales, I shall leave you, and no matter if you're a viscount or not, you will have a wife in name only. I shall make your life a living misery, and do not think I shall not."

He studied her a moment, seeing the truth in her blue eyes. He nodded. "I can agree to those terms." He would do anything if only she looked upon him kindly again. He hated that their marriage was starting on broken dreams and lies. "No matter what you think of me, I do want to make you happy, Isla."

"Hmm," she said, going over to the window and looking out onto the square. "The few months that we were apart, after the house party, what have you been doing with your time? Are there going to be any ladies accosting me at balls throwing snide remarks at me that I have tricked Lord Leigh into matrimony?"

He came over to where she stood, watching her watch the world go by out on the square. "I have not bedded a woman since before the house party in York if that is what you're asking. There has been one particular lady that I cannot get out of my mind."

She did not react to his words, and he wanted to smash that layer of ice she had pulled about her like a cloak where he was concerned. "I hunger for our wedding night, Isla. If you only knew how much I want you. All of you."

For a moment, she did not reply. What was she think-ing? More terrible things that she had no issue telling him to his face. Not that he was feeling sorry for himself, he deserved her wrath, but they would be married and be man and wife. They had to move forward from this rift.

"Is the rest of the house similar in despair as this room?" she asked him, walking over to his desk and running her hand along the wooden top before leaning one hip against it.

"Yes," he shamefully admitted.

"I will start tomorrow ordering new furnishings and furniture. I do not wish to move in here with you in the state that it is in now. Our wedding day will be miserable enough, nevertheless having to come back here and live amongst this squalor."

He came up to her, something he seemed to be doing a lot of. Following her about like a lost puppy. Whatever happened to Lord Leigh, the rake who did whatever he wished? He drank her in and knew what had happened to him. Somewhere and at some time at Lord Billington's house party, he had fallen in love with Miss Isla Woodville. And somehow, she had pivoted to hate him. However were they to return to common ground?

Especially when he still had not been wholly truthful to her.

"Are you going to hate me forever, Isla?" he asked, dreading her answer.

She pursed her lip and sighed. "Quite possibly. I do not like to be used, which I feel has happened. When you thought I was without a sizable dowry, you ignored me after we had been caught alone. That is all I need to know of your character." She pushed past him, striding for the door. "I will see myself out and home. Good day to you, my lord."

CHAPTER
SEVENTEEN

Isla only reached the door handle when a hand moved past her and held the door shut. "I also have terms for our marriage."

She raised one brow, turning to stare up at the man she had wanted with all her heart the moment she had met him at the house party. Only to find out he did not want her in return. Not as a wife in any case. As a lover, she was certain he would have been more than eager, so long as he could have married his rich heiress.

Bile rose in her throat at the thought. And now he had gained all that he wanted, and she couldn't stop the burning anger that thrummed through her each time she thought of the fact.

"I hardly think you're in a position to demand terms, my lord."

"My name is Duke, and no matter the circumstances of how we came to be betrothed, you will marry me, and I will be your husband, and as such, I demand certain favors too if I'm to follow your rules."

Isla leaned against the door. "And those are?" she asked, her tone mocking even to her own ears.

"Do you remember when we first met at Billington's? How well we rubbed along together?"

Heat licked at her skin at the reminder. The decadent kisses that even now threatened to make her toes curl in her slippers. She wanted him still, as angry as she was with the rogue. That they were alone had also not slipped her notice. "Before when you said I was not rich enough for you? Yes, I remember that time well."

His mouth thinned into a displeased line before he said, "Those are my terms. I want what we had then. I want to kiss you whenever and however often I want. I want to bed you." His hand slipped along her waist, squeezing her curves. Her breath hitched as his hand grazed the underside of her breast. "I want to kiss you now. Remind you how good we are together."

Isla swallowed, her body a kaleidoscope of desire and need. She did not want the man in front of her. She hated him for the conniving liar he was, but she also could not deny that she had always been attracted to him. Had wanted him before he hurt her so badly.

"Do as you will," she said in a bored tone while her blood pumped hard and fast in her veins. She may sound nonchalant, but she was anything but. Her body felt afire, ready and aching for him to touch her. Kiss her, do anything he liked to her. She doubted she would protest.

And then, wickedly, he did.

His mouth slammed down on hers, his tongue thrusting against hers, tangling and mating in a dance of desire. She wrapped her arms around his neck, molding her body to his. The time since she had tasted him, kissed him, felt his hands on her body too long. Duke needed no further urging. He lifted her up, carried her over to the settee, and lay her down atop the dust sheet.

Plumes of dust puffed into the air, and she laughed. Her amusement soon faded at the wicked, determined light that entered his eyes. He kneeled at the base of the settee, reaching for her gown and pushing it up her legs. She did not stop him, merely watched under her lashes as she allowed his wickedness.

She loved that he made her warm and ache between her legs. He held her eye as he slipped his hand along her inner thigh, squeezing it every now and then. She shivered, opening farther for him, heedless of the wantonness of her reaction. She did not care. All she wanted was this, him and his clever hands making her shatter into a million delicious pieces.

Isla moaned, biting her lip as his fingers skimmed her mons. "You want me. Feel how wet you are." He touched her there in slow, teasing strokes. She closed her eyes, letting herself simply feel what he did to her.

"So fucking good." The light touch of his lips on her knee startled her. He pushed her knees wider, kissing his way up her thigh, little teasing bites and soothing licks of his tongue as he continued his way up her body.

The blood in her veins pumped hard as his first kiss on her sex rocked through her. She lifted herself off the settee, needing and seeking more of him there. The notion of what he was doing was so unknown and new. She had no idea such a thing was possible, but now all she could think about was what else he would do to her. How wonderful it would feel.

She moaned as his tongue slipped between her folds, lathing her, teasing her in one particular spot she had enjoyed when he had touched her with his hands all those weeks ago.

"You taste so sweet," he growled. "I want to fuck you until you scream my name."

A shiver stole over her body, and she clasped at the settee, fighting to keep herself grounded. "I could eat you every day."

Isla moaned at his filthy discourse. She loved that he enjoyed her so. His tongue flicked her sensitive nubbin before sucking on it. She buckled against him, clasping his head at the wicked sensation that shot through her. "That feels so good, Duke."

He moaned, eating her as if she were the only sustenance he would ever receive again, before he wrenched back, ripping at his front falls. Isla watched him but shook her head. "No, sit back," she said, straddling his waist and placing his hard manhood at her core. "I want to be in control for my first time. I'm going to tup you now, Duke," she said, not sure why she wanted to take charge. So many things between them had happened at his doing. She wanted this one time to be at her undertaking.

"Fuck, Isla," he groaned, his hands squeezing her arse as he teased her cunny against his cock. "I don't want to hurt you. Your first time may be painful, sweetheart," he whispered, kissing her.

"I do not care." She lifted, placing herself over his manhood. He was hard, the size of him making her question her reasoning for only a second before she started to lower herself. She took her time, reveling in the feel of him stretching, melding her in the most intimate of ways.

She watched him, his blue eyes stormy with need. She leaned her forehead against his. Their breaths mingled as their bodies combined. His hands flexed, guided her onto him, and then they were one. For a moment, she did not move, allowing her body to adjust to this new and wonderful sensation and intimacy between them.

"You make me want to come," he gasped when she moved a little, rolling her hips and testing out what she liked and disliked.

She did not dislike much. Nothing, truth be told. She loved the feel of him in her. Isla shifted again, using her knees to stroke up and down on his cock. The sensation was nothing like she had ever felt before. He teased her in a new and wonderous manner. "I want to make you spend," she admitted, knowing that for such a long time, she wanted to be the only person who would be with him in such a way. He was hers, and she would never allow anyone to take what belonged to her.

Just as she knew he would do the same.

"I want so much," she gasped, holding the back of the settee as she rose and fell on his cock. He seemed to grow within her, harder and larger. The need within her spiked. He thrust up into her as she lowered on him. Over and over again, they fucked, and everything between them, all the hurt, the lies, the arguments fell away.

This is what she wanted. This intimacy, this shared pleasure. His hands slipped up her back, holding her shoulders from behind and helping her come down on him. Hard.

"Duke," she moaned, wrapping her arms around his neck. "Don't stop."

"I won't, sweetheart." He increased his pace, her body mindless with pleasure. She could feel the build up within her. Her cunny thrummed with need. He pulled her closer, changing the angle of their joining, and she moaned, his every stroke sparking her to flame. "Duke," she screamed as she toppled over into a void of incandescent pleasure.

Her body convulsed against his cock, draining him, taking all that it could while tremor after tremor shot through every pore, every fiber of her being.

"I'm coming," he groaned, warmth flowing into her body.

They sat for a time, entwined, their breathing labored. Duke met her eye, a wicked smile twisting his lips. "Are you in agreement with my rules, Isla?" he asked her, taking her in a kiss that left her breathless.

She nodded nonsensically. Not quite sure she should agree to anything right at this moment since she still was not thinking clearly. But no matter what, this pleasure, this intimacy she could share with Duke, she knew she could not deny him that. No matter how angry she was at his means of gaining a wife. On this request, at least, they would agree.

CHAPTER
EIGHTEEN

T he preparations for the wedding came together reasonably well over the next few weeks. Her mother took charge along with Hailey and Julia, who had come up with her father when he traveled to London.

The nights were spent at various balls, and never before had Isla been invited out to so many dinners and musical nights. She knew it was because she would soon be Viscountess Leigh, but she did hope a little was because the ladies inviting her to their houses wished for a friendship not solely based on who she would be.

She stood with Lord Leigh at the Davies ball, the Season now well on the way and almost half over. It had been a week since their interlude at his town house, and it had been a week where Isla had trouble concentrating on anything, nevertheless sleeping.

Even now, with Duke towering over her from behind, all she could think about was his hands on her. When he would touch her again. Kiss her even. He had done none of those things, and it was starting to grate. They were to be married in any case. What did it matter if they continued their honeymoon early? She had already slept with him once.

The feel of his finger making a circular pattern at the nape of her neck made her shiver. "Oh," she said, "have you decided to touch me again, my lord? I did not think I warranted another pet since you've been determined this past week to remain distant."

A mocking chuckle sounded at her ear, and she clamped her jaw shut, hating that everything about the man now made her ache with need. His laugh, his smile, his heated glances that went nowhere.

Damn him.

Was he teasing her on purpose?

She had been determined to remain angry with him forever, but she knew she could not. To stay cross took far too much energy, and she wanted to use that effort toward much more fulfilling, enjoyable pastimes.

Like having Duke beneath her again so she could do whatever she wanted with him.

"Are you missing my touch, my love?" he said. Her heart stilled at the word love. Did he mean it, or was it just a benign term of endearment? But she did miss his touch. Now that she had had it in full, she could not get enough of him.

"What would you do if I said that I was?" she asked, meeting his gaze over her shoulder. His mouth twisted into a devious smile, and he stepped closer still, the hardness of his form pressing against her back. "There are things we can do. Places we could disappear to if you wish me to take care of any pressing desires that will not abate."

The very thought of being with him again, of him kissing her, made her wet, and she squirmed, reaching behind her and taking his hand. She started off toward the closest exit. "Come then. Take care of me." Her words were bold, so unlike anything a lady ought to ask, but not her. She had always known to seek what she wanted. Maybe it was the gothic, adventurous, romantic books she read that gave her an unconventional mind, an open and more demanding one, but she would not apologize for it. She wanted him right now, and he would give her what she wanted.

He could not say such things and not mean a word of it.

Duke pulled her to a stop, his chuckle irking her partly. "We cannot leave together, Isla." He glanced about the room. "You leave by the main ballroom doors, head for the retiring room. I shall meet you before you reach your proposed destination."

Isla nodded, expectation thrumming through her at being alone with him again. She headed for the ballroom doors, making her excuses to the few friends who waylaid her, and by the time she started along the upstairs passage toward the retiring room, she could feel Duke's eyes on her. But where was he?

A figure stepped out from behind a curtained window. He flicked his head, telling her to join him without words, and she did without another thought. The moment she stepped into the small window alcove, he was on her. Taking her lips in a searing kiss. Heat and need spiked through her. So much need.

Her legs shook as he turned her roughly, pinning her against the wall. He clasped her hands, placing them above her head, locking them there. "I noticed you like to take control, my love. But do you ever like to relinquish it?"

She frowned, unsure what he meant, but she would let go of everything, her inhibitions, her fears so long as he gave her what she craved. "Yes," she gasped when he reached down, dragging up the back of her gown.

He undulated against her. His breath was warm against her ear, sending a shudder of desire to course through her. Her skin felt aflame, and only his touch could douse it. She pushed back against him, seeking, needing him with a hunger that was beyond reason.

She heard a deep, gravelly growl at her movement. The buttons on his falls ripped open, his hand strong and guiding on her hip. Isla swallowed a moan as the tip of his cock teased her cunny. "Duke, please," she begged him, seeking his fulfillment as if her whole existence relied on it.

"Isla," he sighed, thrusting into her. "You make me lose myself," he gasped into her neck, kissing and nipping it as he took her from behind. His hand came up about her neck, arching her back. "I love fucking you. I have wanted you this past week like I required air. Do not ever think that I do not want you, no matter where we are," he whispered in her ear.

She hummed, loving his words. His hand slipped up her jaw, and he played with her lips with his thumb. "So damn beautiful. Do you know what I want to do with your pretty mouth?" he whispered, his relentless taking of her making her head spin. She clutched at his hand above her on the wall, holding hers, keeping herself from pooling into a puddle of desire at his feet.

"What?" she managed to answer, needing to know.

He growled, slipping two fingers into her mouth. She suckled on them, the salty taste of his skin making her want more. "Your mouth would look good around my cock."

"Mmmm," she agreed, the thought of doing such a

thing now all that she wanted. He pulled his fingers out of her mouth, clasping her hip and angling her in the way that sent her wits to spiral. Her climax hit her without warning, and she buckled against him, thrust back on his cock, and took what her body craved. Her mindless gasps muffled by his kiss.

He pulled out, turning her to face him. Isla lay her hands on his shoulders, wanting him still. "I long to be your husband, Isla," he said, meeting her gaze, his burning with need.

She knew he had not come, and she now also knew she would not leave this alcove without doing what she wanted. She pushed his chest, and he stumbled up against the wall at his back. She kissed her way down his neck, feeling the taut muscles of his abdomen.

Isla kneeled before him, taking in the sight of his manhood, hard and glistening before her. "What do you want me to do with it?" she asked, looking up and meeting his burning-hot gaze. Her body thrummed with expectation at the way he looked at her. As if he wanted to eat her alive in the most delicious way.

"Suck it," he demanded.

She clasped the base of his penis, and it jumped. She smiled, kissing the tip of his cock when a bead of pearl-colored liquid settled there. It was salty, but she liked it. With her tongue, she licked the underside of his manhood, eliciting a moan of pure ecstasy from Duke, and she was lost.

"Oh, I will," she said before taking him fully into her mouth.

. . .

Duke closed his eyes and prayed for redemption. He shouldn't have his cock in his betrothed's mouth at a ball in the middle of London, but also, there was no way in hell he would be pulling out anytime soon.

Her tongue teased its way down his cock before she took him fully into her mouth. He groaned, wanting to clasp her hair, hold her against him and fuck her mouth until he came, but he did not. He allowed the sensation of her sucking him, teasing him with her tongue to lead him on a slow dance to climax.

She was a fast learner, clasping his balls. Her other hand stroked his cock with wicked intent. Her impressive lips locked about his dick with a force that left him reeling. He would come, and soon. He would spend every bit of his pleasure into her willing mouth and enjoy every moment of it.

"Suck me, my love," he breathed, easing farther down her throat. She hummed in agreement, and the vibration was too much. He came, pumping his seed into her mouth like a green lad who could not last. She drank him greedily down, and he could not believe what had happened. How had he been so fortunate to be betrothed to such a spirited, passionate woman? She took his breath away in more ways than one, and he thanked God he had traveled to Lord Billington's estate and had met her.

Fallen in love with her...

The realization struck him, and he pulled her up to stand, staring at her with new, fresh eyes. He was in love with her, of that he could not deny. She smiled at him, a rosy hue kissing her cheeks. He pinned back a curl that had come loose and checked that her gown was all in place.

"Isla, what just happened?" he started, trying to find the words.

She placed a finger against his lips, silencing him. "I loved every moment of it. I only wish that you had shown me sooner how much fun there was to be had behind curtains at balls. Lord Billington's house party might have been a lot more interesting if you had."

He chuckled, pulling her against him. He kissed the top of her head, content to simply hold her. "The moment you tripped on Lord Billington's staircase and landed at my feet, I knew that you would be mine one day. And soon you will be."

She nodded, but the smile on her face slipped a little at his words. She did not believe him. He knew why, but he would make up to her his shortcomings. He would show her with all the years they would be married that he loved and adored her and that she would want for nothing.

"We should return to the ball before we're missed," she said.

He glanced out from the curtain and, seeing the corridor empty, pulled Isla forward. "I will follow in a little while. I shall see you downstairs."

She slipped past him without another word, and he watched her go, the pit of his stomach churning with the lies that still sat between them. His lies that he knew he had to tell her before they were married. He could not marry her without telling her of his mother, of Bedlam, and the rumors that would swirl about London regarding his family's mental stability without giving her a choice to be part of that. He had already taken so much from her. He knew now to marry her and then tell her the truth would be the end of whatever was building between them, and he did not want that.

Even if that meant that he lost the woman he had fallen in love with and the security a marriage to Isla would bring his viscountcy.

If she did not want to marry a man with a mother who had lived half her life in Bedlam, he would have to let her go.

CHAPTER
NINETEEN

Isla woke late the following day after arriving home in the wee hours of the morning. A knock sounded on her door, and she lifted her head, not at all ready to start a new day, when her mama bustled into the room.

"Isla darling, Lord Leigh is here, and he's pacing the library floor. He's asked to speak to you."

She sat up at the mention of Duke being here. Was there something wrong? Had something happened since they parted last evening? She hopped out of bed, her maid Molly helping her dress, who had followed close on her mama's heels.

"Did he say what he is here for?" she asked, picking the light-purple morning gown before reaching for a matching ribbon and tying her hair back.

"You cannot go downstairs with your hair in such a way. You look positively wild."

"I look like a woman who's been pulled out of bed before I wished to by a man who's about to be my husband." Isla went up to her mama, kissing her cheek. "He shall see me in my unmentionables soon enough, mama. I think this is perfectly fine."

Her mama's eyes widened in shock, and she gasped. Isla chuckled and slipped past her, heading for the library.

The moment she stepped into the room, she was wrenched into Duke's arms. He kissed her, taking her lips in an almost desperate way that left her reeling. She wrapped her arms tight about his neck, letting him have his fill of her.

Warmth spread through her at the notion that mayhap he had missed her overnight. That there could be more to their marriage than simply a means to avoid a scandal after being caught together alone. That there could be a chance that her marriage could turn into a union of affection, maybe even love. Not just his love for her money.

Isla pulled back, grinning. "What was that kiss for, my lord? We only parted," she said, glancing at the clock on the mantle, "four hours ago."

He wrapped his arm about her waist and walked her to the settee. "I needed to speak to you. See you. Tonight was too many hours away."

They sat on the settee, and he took her hand, meeting her eye. "We're to be married soon, and I wanted to speak to you alone. Your mama allowed it, but there are some things that you need to know about me, Isla."

More things than she already knew? What else had he not told her? She sat back, a chill running down her spine. "There is more that you need to tell me about your life?" she asked, her stomach rioting.

Duke swallowed, a sheen of sweat beaded on his brow. "No, I merely meant that I wanted to discuss that although our marriage came about by unconventional means, that does not mean that I do not want to make our marriage a happy one. I know I do not want to spend my life miserable, and well, after last evening, we do seem to get along very well."

Isla moved closer, needing to touch him. She laid her hand on his leg and felt him jump at her touch. "I enjoyed last evening too." She ran her hand along his thigh until she skimmed the hardness in his pants.

She felt herself grow wet and needy for him, her cunny aching with renewed want. A muscle worked in his jaw as she pressed harder, stroking his manhood until it bulged against his falls. "I want you even now, Duke," she admitted.

He clasped her jaw, kissing her hard. A moan passed his lips as she tightened her hold on his phallus. "We could be caught at any moment. Your father could return to use his library."

"Don't you want me?" she teased, pouting for good measure. She knew he did. And from the size of his manhood, he wanted her just as much as she did him. Isla ached, needing him to make her feel as wonderful as he had last evening. She straddled his lap, and he shook his head.

"No, Isla, we'll be caught, and your parents will literally kill me before I have a chance to make you my wife."

"Then be quick about it," she teased. Her request for them to be together now, here in her family's London home, was absurd. But so too was the need that ricocheted through her. She needed him, knew that if she did not have him now, her day would be one of frustration. And she had things to do today, wedding preparations and ordering gowns for her trousseau. She could not be irritable.

Duke clasped Isla's hips like a lifeline. He could not fuck her in her father's library when at any moment anyone could enter. It was madness, yet that emotion overtook his senses and made him reckless.

He was a rogue and one hell-bent on going to the underworld for his actions. Before he could change his mind, he ripped open his falls and guided her down onto him. She sighed against his lips. He clamped his jaw, fighting to remain calm, not flip her over on the settee and thrust into her like some green lad on his first foray into the world of gratification.

She smelled divine, of roses and something else uniquely her. Her lilac gown made the blue of her eyes sparkle with mischief. She would be the end of him. He'd come here to tell her of his mother, to give her a choice to marry him or not.

He had not come here to fuck her, even if a part of him had hated that the night before had ended, and he had returned to his home alone. He wanted her with him, beside him. To be able to love her as he now did whenever they wished.

"Duke," she whimpered. The sound of her desire, the frustration and the need that thrummed through her voice undid him. He flipped her onto the settee and thrust into her with such force she cried out.

She slapped a hand over her mouth, her other holding the end of the settee as he relentlessly took her. Adrenaline rushed through his blood, along with need. The feel of her first convulsions about his cock dragged his release along with hers, and he came hard, pumping his seed into her without thought.

His breathing ragged, he pulled out, righting himself in

his breeches and wrenching her up off the settee to settle her gowns about her ankles just at the door to the library opened, and Isla's mother walked in with a maid carrying refreshments.

"I thought you both may need a light repast," Mrs. Woodville said, smiling at them both.

Duke dared not look at his attire in fear that something was amiss. He did, however, glance at Isla, who sat on the settee as if all was as it should be. Not as if they had just had sex like a pair of rutting animals. He ought to be ashamed, be on his knees begging for forgiveness for being such a cad.

But all he could think of was when he would have her again. She was like an addiction he could not wean himself from. Their marriage would not be one of convenience. Not for him, at least. The woman looking up at him as if she were the meaning of innocence itself meant everything to him. He loved her and could not say no to her.

And he could no longer lie to her. She had to know the truth from him before another day passed. He would do it tonight when they were once again alone and give her a choice. He just hoped she would choose him.

CHAPTER

TWENTY

I sla walked into her sister's ball, now the Duchess of Derby, and slipped her cloak from her shoulders, handing it to a liveried footman. The house on Berkeley Square was one of the finest in London, and she looked up the stairs to see her sister and the duke greeting a long line of guests.

"How well Hailey looks, Mama," she mentioned to her mother, who stood at her side. Julia too had come tonight since this was a family-held ball, and not too many people would naysay the duke and duchess, and certainly not at their own event.

They made their way up the stairs before paying their regards to their hosts.

"I'm so happy you are here. Thank you for coming tonight," Hailey said, kissing her mama first before hugging both Isla and Julia in turn.

"The house smells divine and looks wonderful. We cannot wait to see the ballroom and dance the night away," Isla said, bussing the duke's cheeks before they moved on into the ballroom.

The room was already a crush. What looked to be hundreds of people stood about, talking and drinking glasses of wine and champagne. "There is Lord Leigh. Let us go to him so you may have your first dance with your betrothed," her mama said, pulling her toward Duke.

Isla took the opportunity to drink him in as they moved ever closer to where he stood with several gentlemen, most of whom had been at Lord Billington's for the house party. Several of the men whom Isla knew were privy to Duke's wishes when it came to his wife.

"Isla, darling," Duke said, picking up her gloved hand and kissing it before placing it on his arm. "I'm glad that you're here," he said, meeting her eye, a devilish light sparkling in his blue ones.

"We are happy to have found you, my lord," her mama answered for all of them. "What a crush this night looks to be."

Several of the gentlemen agreed before they returned to their conversation. "But a merry one," Lord Leigh stated, winking at Isla and Julia. He leaned down toward her ear. "I have missed you this afternoon. I cannot get you out of my mind."

Heat coursed through her at the mention of what they had done in the library of her home. Reckless, dangerous, such silliness that she still could not believe they had partaken in such activity, but they had. A quick tumble she supposed she could term it, and never had she felt such satisfaction. Never had she wanted to do what they had both enjoyed as much as she did right now.

"There is a conservatory on the opposite side of the house. It's some distance from the ball, and I doubt many know the house has one. We could meet there. Be alone for a time," she whispered.

Duke glanced about the room, noting her mother's and sister's whereabouts. "Do you think you will be able to? With your mother and sister here, will they not miss you if you leave?"

"Not if I slip away after a dance. They will think that I have moved to another group of friends to converse with."

"Very well," he agreed before pulling her out onto the dance floor as the first dance of the ball was about to commence. "First, however, I must have you in my arms," he teased, enjoying the smile that lit up her beautiful face. He swallowed hard, the knowledge that he was going to tell her the truth this evening, all of his truth, left him riddled with unease.

Would she be angry? Would she ask for the marriage contracts to be canceled? All things she could do, and he would let her, for he needed her to marry him as much as he wanted to marry her for the right reasons. Not because someone told them to because they were caught, or because he needed her money.

But because he loved her, as much as he hoped she loved him.

They danced a set comprised of three dances, and by the time they moved to the side of the room where a footman promptly handed them a glass of punch, they were both breathing hard from the exertion.

"That was fun," Isla said, sipping her drink. "You are a very fine dancer, Lord Leigh. Has anyone ever told you such?" she asked him.

He shook his head, certain they had not. "No, not that I can remember." He moved them farther away from the dance floor. "What other things do I do well, Miss Woodville? Does anything come to mind?" he teased.

She raised one brow, her eyes darkening with understanding. "There are other things, of course, you are particularly good at. Shall we walk and discuss the matter further?" she asked him.

"Yes," he agreed, not bothering to slip away unnoticed tonight. He walked with Isla out of the room and toward the back of the house. Isla whispered the direction, and they came across no one, not even servants, before they arrived at the conservatory, the moonlit night lighting the room from above.

"Does it not smell divine?" she said, walking into the thick foliage of the plants. He followed. The room was so densely populated with flowers and ferns that it would not take much to lose one in such space.

"Not as divine as you do, my darling," he admitted. Her scent would forever be his favorite.

She threw an impish look over her shoulder before sitting on a stone bench. "You wanted to talk to me, and I gather that it is the same thing you wished to discuss today at my home before we ah...became distracted."

He sat beside her, thrusting the thought of what they had done today out of his mind. He needed to concentrate, not lust after her even more than he did already. "It is the same matter." He kissed her quickly, needing to taste her one more time lest she banish him from her life forever after this evening.

She clasped his hand, squeezing it a little. "Considering what I know of you already and your plans on gaining a wife, I do not think you need to look as worried as you do," she said, her eyes bright.

Never in his life did Duke hate himself as much as he did right at this moment. Trying to find a rich bride was nothing compared to what he kept from her still. "Isla," he began, steeling himself to be strong. "Many years ago, when I was just a boy and did not notice such things, my father sent my mother away. It was all very hush-hush from what I can gather, and no one spoke of it to me even when I came of age. My father passed away two years past, and on his deathbed, he revealed something to me that I think you ought to know."

"Me?" she said, pointing to herself. "Why do I need to know such things? Is that not a private matter between you and your papa?" she asked him. She was so innocent, not able to imagine the horror he was about to bestow on her.

"My father sent my mother away to Spain and had her institutionalized for mental deficiencies, I believe. He thought she was not of sound mind and did not want her near his son and heir where he may be put in danger."

Isla's eyes widened, and she paled to a ghostly shade of gray. "Madness runs in your family? Is that what you're trying to say?" she asked, her voice trembling at the words.

"I do not believe so. I think he sent her away to be cruel. It was not a happy marriage, and he believed her to be unfaithful. That is what I was able to gather from some staff who worked for my father at the time. But I cannot prove it, not until I have someone go to Spain and see for themselves. I would like to bring her back to England. To where she belongs."

"To live here with you in England. With us, if we marry?" she stated, looking at him as if he had sprouted two heads. "Why did you not tell me this before? I think knowing lunacy runs in your family should have been something I was told of before our betrothal was announced."

Duke sat back, disappointment lodging in his gut. "We were caught alone. There was little choice in announcing our betrothal. As for my mother's mental wellbeing, you know I could not tell you such a thing, not until we were either engaged or married. If it became known about London that my mother has been locked up in Bedlam these past twenty years, no heiress looking for a title would have taken a second look in my direction. I cannot afford to free her without the funds from my future bride, as much as that pains me to admit."

Isla stood, pacing several steps from him. "And what will happen to our children should your mother be returned to you and she is suffering from some kind of break in the mind? We will be shunned, and our children will never be looked upon as a good match, that is what. How could you have used me in such a way to get what you wanted?"

"I had to, Isla," he said, coming up to her. "Because to tell such a thing to any of the ladies I courted, I would have had the same reaction you are having now. But I care for you," he said, clasping her upper arms. "I did not want you to go into this marriage without knowing this of me. Of my heritage. I want you to choose me because I am who you want, no matter the noise that brought us together. Just as I want to marry you for who you are and how you make me feel."

She shook her head, wrenching from his hold. "The stigma of such an illness, whether true or not, will cling, and we shall all suffer for it. This does not just affect you, but my sisters too. They may be looked down upon from mere association." She set her hands on her hips, clearly debating what she had found out. A shock, Duke knew, but one he had to tell her. He could not keep this from her too. Had he told her this after their marriage, she would never have trusted him ever again.

"Do you ever suffer within your own thoughts? Do you believe this to be true of your mother? Do you think you too will have some sort of break of the mind in the future?"

"No," he snapped, hating where her deliberations were headed. "I have never been melancholy or had bouts of manic behavior, and I do not believe my mother did either."

"And what makes you so sure?" she asked, turning to face him. "You were but a child."

"My father apologized about my mother before he took his last breath. Why would he do that unless he felt guilt over the matter? Mayhap even guilt that he had placed her there when she did not deserve to be so."

"Your father's words may have meant something else entirely, and you are hoping for an outcome that is never going to come true." She paused, chewing her bottom lip. "What have you done to seek answers? Surely you have sent someone to Spain now that your future financials have been secured by me."

He cringed, hating that he had and that she was right. That he had more options now that he was about to marry a rich heiress. "I am waiting on news from a runner I hired to travel there and find the answers I seek. I sent him before I left for the Billington Estate." She glanced up at him, and he understood the question in her eyes. "I was certain, you see, that I would marry an heiress and soon. I had little choice in the matter, a shameful act, but one I cannot apologize any further for than I have already."

"And if news from Spain comes back and it is not to your liking, what will you do then? What will we do?" she asked him. "Am I to marry you still with this dark cloud hanging over our future?"

"It is not true, Isla. I'm certain of it." He took a calming breath, searching for the correct words. "Is such illness so unpalatable to you that you could not marry me even knowing this of my mother?"

"Well, even if it were, I have little choice in the matter since you decided to follow me into the lady's retiring room, taking that choice from me," she bit back at him, her voice hard.

"I was not the only one who was eager for more kisses," he threw at her, hating that they were arguing over this at all. Not to mention he hated that he was wrong in many ways. It was him who had followed her. He had taken her choices away from her. And now again, he was forcing his mother's possible lunacy on her too. Expecting her to be accepting of such news. He strode over to the circular fountain, staring at the cupid spilling water from his mouth. "Will you still marry me knowing this of my family?" he asked her, praying that she would and not because he needed her money but because he could no longer see a future without her in it.

She was a calming influence on him, made him feel things he had never felt before in his life, and he could not see himself with anyone else. Not ever.

"You know that I cannot break a contract when it was fashioned out of scandal. I would not do such a thing to my family twice. I was lucky that we did not suffer more than a few snark remarks from the *ton*. We could have been given the cut direct."

Relief poured through him, and he schooled his features when he noticed her watching him. "I'm sorry, Isla."

She shook her head, disappointment shadowing her blue eyes. "Yes, you keep saying that to me, Lord Leigh. So much so that it has become repetitive," she said, leaving him in the conservatory with only his shame for company.

CHAPTER
TWENTY-ONE

"Oh my dear, this is terrible news!" her mother all but screeched as she strode into the breakfast room the following morning, *The Times* in hand, which she was flapping about like a loose bird with its feet trapped.

"What is it, my love?" her father asked, placing his coffee cup down before picking up his fork.

"The news in the paper. It's about Lord Leigh. He's ruined. This paper states that he has no money, nothing to his name."

"I already know this of the man. What else is there to know?" her father said, throwing a cursory glance at Isla.

She pursed her lips, not willing to divulge anything about Lord Leigh to her parents or anyone else. His family was her burden, and she would not allow anyone else to suffer under such weight. The word Bedlam banged about in her mind, and she could not help but be troubled about it. What it would mean for them in the years to come. The severity his mother suffered with, if indeed she were afflicted. And would that disease manifest in Lord Leigh at some time in his life, would their children suffer the same fate? Oh, the concerns were endless.

"It is stated in the article that his mother, who everyone presumed had run off from Viscount Leigh when the young heir was just a child, never ran off at all. An unnamed source said last evening they overheard Lord Leigh himself state that his mother could have possibly been sent away to Spain due to a sickness of mind and has possibly been incarcerated in a hospital for lunacy."

Her father's cutlery clattered onto the table, and Isla swallowed the bile that rose in her throat. Someone must have been in the conservatory with them and had heard everything. This means they knew their marriage was also not one of affection and love but because they were indeed caught together alone at the Collins ball.

She would be shamed and ignored in society. Even if she did marry Lord Leigh and save his financial woes, there would be little left for them in London. Especially now that his family's dark secret was also revealed to the world.

A knock sounded on the dining room door, and their butler entered. "Viscount Leigh is here to see you, Miss Woodville."

"Send him in here," her father said, pushing away his meal and dabbing his mouth with the napkin.

Her mother sent her a worried glance before Lord Leigh strode into the room, the dark circles beneath his eyes telling her he had not slept since returning home from the ball last evening. Not after reading the article.

"Good morning," his lordship said, bowing a little. "I apologize for the early morning call, but I thought it best that I come here today." He gestured to the paper her mama held against her chest like a shield. "I see you have read the latest scandal that is right at this moment waking all of London and revealing my family's woes."

Her father cleared his throat. "We have read about the dowager viscountess, and we're sorry for your troubles, Lord Leigh, but this is something I believe you ought to have disclosed to me prior to asking my daughter for her hand."

Lord Leigh seemed to gather himself before he said, "There are many things that I ought to have done differently, Mr. Woodville. But alas, I am human and am not immune to mistakes." He paused, meeting Isla's eyes. "With this information about my family now common knowledge, I know that you cannot marry me. It would not be fair for me to hold you to our understanding, considering the disease that possibly runs through my blood and any children we were to sire. I cannot have such a tragedy befall you too or those close to you who may partake in this downfall by association."

"You compromised my daughter, Lord Leigh. I think it is a little too late to try to persuade Isla to break ties with you," her father stated, his voice harder than Isla had ever heard before.

"I think you will find, sir, that with the scandal of my mother and that last evening it was also revealed with certainty that I'm without funds, that no one will remember how it came about that we were engaged. My name will be worthless by this evening, and it is best for Isla and her sisters that we part now and have no further contact between us."

The pit of Isla's stomach twisted in dread at the thought of what was happening. Of what Lord Leigh was saying. She could understand, and she would be lying if she stated that his words did not bring a little relief that she would not have to marry him. They were not a union made out of love and affection, which is what she had wanted.

But now, to be separated from him, to know that she would never be with him again, talk to him, have him kiss her until she forgot her own sense and time was not comforting either.

This whole situation was a mess.

"We will make it known this evening then, my lord, that the understanding has come to an end."

Duke met her eyes, and she saw the pain that swirled within his. He was hurting from all of this. And now that he had lost her and her fortune, he would hurt even further. "Are you attending Lord Billington's ball this evening?" Isla asked.

He nodded. "It will be my last before I return to my country estate. Billington is one of my closest friends, and I shall not disappoint him, but that is all." He bowed. "Thank you again for seeing me. Good day to you all," he said, and he was gone.

Isla wanted to run after him, talk to him, see if it were really as bad as he thought it was. Surely it was not. Not without proof of his mother's illness, what really could anyone say.

A great deal, she would later find out...

Duke returned to his town house and found his servants busily packing and closing up the house for his return to Hampshire. He strode into his library, slumping down on the settee, his mind a whirl of thoughts. Most of them despondent and worrying.

He had not wanted to let go of Isla, but it was for the best, for her in any case. He could not marry her and bring her down along with him. Families with those affected in mind with lunacy were not the type of people the beau monde wanted to include in their social spheres or their heritage. She would thank him one day when she found the man who loved her and she in return. A man without so many secrets in his closet.

He ran a hand over his face. The runner he had sent to Spain would return, and then he would need to figure out how to pay the remainder of his fee. Without Isla, that was now an impossibility. Unless he sold this house, something he was loath to do.

"Damn it", he swore, thumping the settee with his fists, not that the outburst of emotion made him feel any better or changed his fate.

He was ruined, and tonight at the Billington ball, everyone would partake in his downfall, including the woman he loved.

CHAPTER
TWENTY-TWO

The Billington ball was a crush, everyone who was anyone in the *ton* was present, and Isla wasn't fool enough not to know why. They were here to hang one of their own, to watch him squirm and wither under their silk-slippered feet when they trod on him.

Isla had not wanted to attend. She did not want to be part of what was going to happen, and the sense of trepidation and expectation was thick in the air.

They made their way into the ball, and Isla went and stood near her sister Hailey and the duke who had arrived before them. She kissed her sister's cheek, dipping into a curtsy before them both. "I'm so thankful you are here. I think tonight I shall need your support."

"Of course, sister," Hailey said, throwing her a concerned look. "Mama sent a note over this afternoon explaining what was happening. Is it true that Lord Leigh has asked you to end your understanding? That he has a mother, who has been hospitalized in Spain for lunacy since he was a child?"

Isla nodded, taking a glass of punch from a passing

footman. "Indeed it is true, all of it, unfortunately." She drank down a good portion. "He is going to be here tonight, but I fear for how he will be treated."

"Hmm," her sister murmured. "What do you think of it all?" she asked her.

Isla opened her mouth to reply but closed it as Lady Francesca, Lady Susan, and Lady Martha joined them. Each of them reached out to take Isla's hand, their faces one of compassion.

"Oh, dearest Miss Woodville. How sorry we are for you. To be caught up in the scandalous behavior of Lord Leigh is positively horrendous," Lady Francesca said.

Lady Susan nodded eagerly. "To think that each of us was courted by the man. And all the while, he was looking for a rich bride to stop his pockets from being let. I'm disgusted that you, Miss Woodville, were his victim in the end."

"I have little doubt," Lady Martha added, "that his following you into the retiring room was planned all along. That he needed his rich bride to fill his empty coffers and to seek out his mother, and you being so innocent and unaware of the rules in town made you easy prey for him."

The sick feeling that Isla had been living with all day returned with a vengeance, and she thought she may be ill. She took a deep breath, striving to calm herself. Mumbles and gasps sounded, and Isla looked toward the door and saw Lord Leigh enter the room with Lord Billington.

He did not appear like a man who was ruined. A man whom everyone now knew all his family's secrets. And yet Isla could see in his eyes that they were haunted, shuttered, and on guard.

"How dare he make an appearance here. The man has

no shame," Lady Martha said, distaste twisting her normally pretty mouth.

"His mother is a lunatic from what I have heard, and we all know that deficiency runs in bloodlines. He is as tainted as one possibly can be. No one will marry him now, even if he does come with a title." Lady Francesca turned up her nose, pleased with her cutting remark.

"A viscountess is not as well as we can do, ladies," Lady Susan said. "I think we ought to agree that nothing below an earl will do for us."

The other ladies nodded in agreement, their amused but vindictive gazes swinging back to Lord Leigh.

He stood with several gentlemen, but his gaze was on Isla. She could see the pain, the shame that thrummed through him, and she hated that he was alone and had no one.

Anger replaced her silence, and she refused to allow a moment longer of her time listening to their sharp barbs. "If I remember correctly, Lady Susan, you were more than happy to gain the title of viscountess at Lord Billington's country house party. In fact, if memory serves me right, you were quite the tease with his lordship in the hopes that he would pick you out of you three."

Each of the ladies gasped, and Isla's sister Hailey clasped her arm, laughing awkwardly. "I think my sister means to say..." she began, but Isla wasn't having a notion of it.

"We do not even know for certain if Lord Leigh's mama is troubled of mind, and there is no medical certainty that such illness is passed along to children," she added. Unsure of that fact but not willing to allow the three vultures before her to slander Lord Leigh over situations that were not his fault.

"Furthermore, the ills of one's parents is not something any of us can alter. Lord Leigh's father, from what I know, squandered the money and left his son with very nearly nothing to keep the houses and those staffed within them running. I think Lord Leigh ought to be commended for his diligence in trying to keep himself afloat. He could have, as so many young men have in the past, drunk himself into a stupor or married women like you and lived miserable, loveless, passionless lives for the remainder of their days."

Her brother-in-law, the duke, raised his glass in a toast. "Now that is something I shall toast to, Isla," he said, winking at her.

Hailey chuckled, and Isla grinned at them both, happy to have their support.

"How dare you speak to us in such a way, Miss Woodville. Do you know who we are and what we can do to you in society?"

The duke cleared his throat, stepping forward. "I would suggest you do nothing to my wife's sister unless each of you wish to die old maids and wards of your brothers who shall inherit the bulk of your family's money. If you threaten Isla, you threaten the Duke of Derby. Do I make myself clear?"

Each of the ladies gaped, their mouths opening and closing like a fish out of water. "We meant, Your Grace, that Viscount Leigh is ruined. Look at him, sad and alone, penniless and without options. He is sunk and will sink further still. No friendship of the duke will save him," Lady Francesca said, malice in her tone. "Even with a title on offer of viscountess, few if any will want it if his mother is mad and therefore mayhap even himself in time."

"And no one wishes to marry a horse," Isla said, wanting to hurt Lady Francesca at her cruel words toward a man she loved. And she did love him and wanted him still, even with all the troubles he faced.

He had given her up, let her go to make a future reminiscent of the one she had told him she dreamed of when they first met. A marriage of love and affection, passion and friendship. He had let her go, used his own downfall and disgrace to enable her to slip free. He could have held her to their understanding. He could have married her no matter what rumors circulated in London.

But he had not.

She glanced over to him, pushing past the three ladies who stumbled out of her way. Hailey called after her, but she ignored everyone, her sole purpose Duke. With each step toward him, her body came to life, thrummed with purpose and determination. He had let her go, but that did not mean she wanted to be set free.

Not by him. She loved him, all of him and all that he was to face. She did not want him to do it alone. She wanted to be by his side, holding his hand and tackling all the scary, sad, and nasty things life could throw at them together.

She wanted him, and nothing would keep her from getting what she wanted. Just as the heroines in her books were strong and brave, she would be too. And by doing so, get all that her heart desired.

Duke could not tear his eyes from Isla as she came toward him, an Amazonian goddess whose determined strides and eyes that glowed with the same emotion came ever closer.

His heart stopped at the sight of her, so beautiful and

marvelous, strong and brave. Hope rose within him that her coming toward him meant that what he felt for the woman who had captured his heart and soul, everything that made him who he was, felt the same in return.

She stepped before him, and he ignored the fact that the ball had come to a stop, that people were watching, waiting for the interaction between them to play out.

They were hoping for a public set down, he knew, and damn it all to hell, he deserved one, but he could not help but pray it would never come. That she was before him, beautiful as ever because she loved him. That she disagreed with his ending their understanding.

His attention dipped to her lips, and he had never wanted to kiss a woman as much as he wanted to kiss Isla right at this moment.

"Lord Leigh," she started, a small smile lifting her lips. "About our conversation this morning."

"Yes," he answered her, praying he was right, what he felt was true. "You wish to discuss the matter further?"

She nodded, handing her glass of punch to a footman not far from them before taking his hands. "When you mentioned today that you were setting me free of our understanding, you did not give me a chance to respond."

Which was indeed true, he had not, but he had thought her silence answer enough. That his offer to end their betrothal was welcome. "And you wish to respond now?" he asked her.

"I do wish to speak on what you suggested, only to tell you that I do not agree. I do not want to be freed from our understanding. I do not want to marry anyone else but you, you see. From the moment I stumbled at your feet, I, too, felt as though our lives would be entwined in some way. At least I hoped they would be, and I do not want to now be with anyone else but you. I love you, you see."

Gasps sounded about them, and he ignored them all. Wanting only to hear Isla's voice.

"I love all of you, even the messy bits." She smiled, and he chuckled, his hands squeezing hers, keeping her locked before him.

"You love me? Even though my mother may be a lunatic? Even though I hunted fortunes before your nose?" he asked, the sound of his sins making him inwardly cringe.

"Whatever the future holds with the dowager viscountess, we shall deal with it together, as husband and wife, and not allow any of the *ton* to make a fuss over something that has nothing to do with them."

Her words made his heart thump hard in his chest. How was he so fortunate to have met her? She was magnificent.

"As for your fortune-hunting, I think I have chastised you enough regarding that. I understand that men need something to live on as much as the ladies long for titles. I was naive to think that people had more sense than to sell themselves to such futures. But our future will be different, for I love you and will gladly share my life and wealth with you so long as you marry me and love me forever."

Duke had heard enough. His throat felt thick, and he found swallowing hard. He wrenched her into his arms and kissed her. He forgot where they were and merely lost himself in the feel of Isla back in his arms.

She felt like home, soft and warm, the rose perfume that she often wore seeping into his senses like a drug. The desperation in their kiss was too much and yet not enough. He wanted more. Much more. A lifetime of this. Her. Them.

"I will marry you," he said, pulling back, pushing a lock of hair off her cheek to sit behind her ear. "And I promise never to keep anything from you again. You are the other half to my soul, and I never wish to be parted from you."

She slipped her arms about his neck. "Do you think we could have the wedding brought forward? Two weeks seems like a lifetime to wait," she suggested.

"I shall procure a special license, and we will be man and wife within a day."

"That sounds perfect," she said.

He dipped his head, needing to kiss her again. "I whole-heartedly agree," he said, before he did exactly that.

EPILOGUE

Madrid, Spain

Isla stared at the estate's name that the runner had given Duke as to the viscountess's whereabouts in Spain. She looked at Duke, who had the same confused, swindled appearance that she knew she sported. Bedlam? Was the institution some sort of foolery? Making a mockery toward those who suffered?

They walked along the graveled drive, spying several people working out in the gardens. Isla narrowed her eyes, unable to remove the feeling of dread that had settled in her stomach. What was this place? The openness of the yard, the non-guarded gate. It was not how she thought an institution would run to keep those within its care safe from the outside world, which they may not understand.

An older gentleman with graying hair came out onto the front steps, shading his eyes to see who it was that was visiting. Isla smiled at the stranger, hoping it may help them gain answers before they were run off from the place.

"Lord Leigh, I would recognize you anywhere," the

older man stated as if he had been expecting him. "You look like the dowager viscountess."

Duke flinched at the statement, and Isla took his arm, feeling for him. This would not be an easy reunion if they were to have one. "I've come to see the dowager viscountess if she's up for visitors and if it is allowed here. We were unsure of the rules of Bedlam."

The older man threw him a confused glance before gesturing them into the house. "Come this way. Her ladyship is on the back terrace." They walked through the Spanish-inspired home. The marble floors and tapestries on the wall made the house feel cooler than the day outside. A welcome reprieve in the endless heat that was Spain.

They stepped out onto the terrace, and Isla spied a woman dressed in a white, flowing gown and scarf about her hair. She gasped. There was no mistaking Duke and his mother shared the same blood, even from this position.

The older woman looked to see who had arrived, and her smile faded to one of shock. She stood, her chair scraping on the stone terrace as she did so. Isla let go of Duke and watched with a lump in her throat as mother and child reunited after many years.

"Duke?" the woman asked, wonder in her voice.

Isla bit her lip, trying to stem the tears that seemed to want to run profusely all of a sudden.

"Mother?" Duke asked in return, disbelief in his tone. "You are not mad?" he blurted.

The viscountess raised her brow, her eyes wide before she burst out laughing, striding toward her child. "No, why on earth would you think such a thing?" She took her son's hands, inspecting him as if he were a newborn babe laid in her arms. "I cannot believe you are here. How did you find me?"

"A runner," Duke said. He pulled Isla forward, and his mother turned her attention on her. "This is my wife, Isla. We were married during the past Season in town."

Duke's mother smiled at Isla, and warmth radiated from her. Isla wasn't sure what she expected upon meeting the dowager viscountess, but sanity and warmth were not it.

"It is lovely to meet you, Isla, and to see you again, my son. It has been too many years." Her ladyship invited them to sit, and they joined her on the terrace. "I suppose you have many questions, and I too, as I did not ever think to see you again."

Duke frowned at his mother's words, and Isla knew they made little sense to him. He'd been led to believe she had been locked away, banished from England. Was any of that true at all?

"Why were you in Spain all these years and not beside my father in England? On his deathbed, he told me you were here but in Bedlam. I assumed that he meant..."

"That I was of unsound mind?" His mother laughed, but the sound wasn't at all joyful. "He should never have married me. He wanted me for my fortune, and that was all. By marrying me, he came into funds prior to his father's passing, and that was all he cared about. Certainly not me or you when we were blessed with your arrival." Her ladyship sighed, looking out over her Spanish gardens, the sound of tinkling water masking the silence. "He never wanted a wife and was soon bored with me. I became a nuisance in his life, so he did what so many men of his ilk do when they no longer wish to be married to a woman they do not love.

"They say they're of unsound mind and put them away in an institution. Lucky for me, my prison was Spain, and my loyal servant Manis refused to follow through on your father's wishes to have me put away for the rest of my life. I have a small allowance from my paternal grandmother that enables me to rent this villa, and we named it Bedlam. We were reckless, you see, for going against your father's wishes, and we thought the name fitting. Now that he told you of my home here in Spain, I wonder if he knew all along."

Isla couldn't help but think that mayhap he did. She glanced at Duke and could see all of this information was new to him. She reached out, taking his face in her hands. "Duke, what your father told you is untrue. Your mama is not in Bedlam. She merely made fun of your father wanting her institutionalized by naming her home such. Nothing more."

He took her hands, kissing them quickly. "I thought you were a lunatic. All of London believes that is so."

Her ladyship chuckled, shaking her head. "Now that your father is gone, I will return to London and take up my duties as the dowager viscountess, and I shall prove to everyone that they are wrong about me and the rumors my husband spread. I will not allow my son's name to be shadowed by such untruths or the future of our family through your marriage." She sighed, shaking her head. "I should have returned sooner. I should not have left you at all, but I had no choice. Not many women do when faced with what I had to live through."

His mother glanced at Isla's stomach, and she moved her hand away from the precious gift she carried within her. "How far along are you, my dear?"

Isla gaped, hopeful but not certain that she was with child.

"You're *enceinte*?" Duke asked her, shock rippling across his face as he stood.

Isla shrugged, joining him. "I do not know for certain, but I'm late for my courses. I did not want to say anything without being sure." She turned to the dowager viscountess. "How did you suspect?" she asked, feeling Duke's arms slide about her waist.

"You're practically glowing, my dear, and a woman knows these things. We're special that way."

Duke chuckled. "I cannot believe it. We're having a child?" He took a deep breath. "Oh, my darling Isla. I cannot believe how fortunate I am."

"I can," his mother said, summoning a servant. "Champagne for us all, thank you. I would like to celebrate with my son and new daughter the forthcoming birth of my grandchild."

Duke glanced at his mother, a question in his eyes. "Why did you never return to England? I could have used your support and guidance. Father was never very present. He was not unkind, just indifferent."

"Had I returned, he would have had his wish, and I would have been locked away somewhere in England where he had more power. I did not want to leave you, but I also knew you were better off in England. You were the heir, and for all your father's faults, he would not do anything to put your life in danger."

"Other than leaving the viscountcy without a penny to its name," he added.

His mother looked at him, displeased. "I knew your father would do that. It was written in his book of life long before I married him that he could not economize."

Isla squeezed Duke's hand.

"But alas, my son, look at you now. You have a beautiful, loving wife. Marrying Isla and loving her as much as I suspect you do, makes you wealthier than anyone in the world, does it not?"

"Well, I will not disagree, your ladyship," Isla said, smiling.

Duke met her eyes. His a storm of emotions, love, pride, hunger. All the wonderful things she loved making him feel. "Never have I heard truer words spoken," he agreed, dipping his head and kissing her softly. "I am lucky she chose me, for I would be poor indeed without her."

Isla bit her lip, wanting to tease him. "Well, you would have been both poor of heart and of pocket, but thankfully my heart was persuaded otherwise."

"Have I told you how glad I am that you're so independent and tenacious?" he asked her. "And of independent thinking."

"There was a time when you thought those features a deficit," she reminded him, some of their first disagreements coming to mind.

"Not anymore. Not even then," he admitted.

Isla leaned up and kissed him in return. "I love you too, Duke," she whispered for only him to hear, just as a footman brought out the champagne for all of them to drink. They toasted to their future family with love and happiness. And finally, she had become a heroine of her own love story that included scandal, betrayal, secrets, and a passionate love affair. She could not have asked for a better ending to her tale than the one she was given. She could only hope their next adventure was just as exciting, and from the wicked look in Duke's eyes, she knew it very soon would be.

Dear Reader

T hank you for taking the time to read *On a Wild Duke Chase*! I hope you enjoyed the second book in my Wayward Woodvilles series!

I'm forever grateful to my readers, and if you're able, I would appreciate an honest review of *On a Wild Duke Chase*. As they say, feed an author, leave a review!

Alternatively, you can keep in contact with me by visiting my website, subscribing to my newsletter or following me online. You can contact me at www.tamarag-ill.com.

Happy reading!

Tamara Gill

The Wayward Woodvilles

Series starts Feb, 2022
Pre-order your copy today!

SERIES BY TAMARA GILL

The Wayward Woodvilles

Royal House of Atharia

League of Unweddable Gentlemen

Kiss the Wallflower

Lords of London

To Marry a Rogue

A Time Traveler's Highland Love

A Stolen Season

Scandalous London

High Seas & High Stakes

Daughters Of The Gods

Stand Alone Books

Defiant Surrender

To Sin with Scandal

Outlaws

ABOUT THE AUTHOR

Tamara is an Australian author who grew up in an old mining town in country South Australia, where her love of history was founded. So much so, she made her darling husband travel to the UK for their honeymoon, where she dragged him from one historical monument and castle to another.

A mother of three, her two little gentlemen in the making, a future lady (she hopes) and a part-time job keep her busy in the real world, but whenever she gets a moment's peace she loves to write romance novels in an array of genres, including regency, medieval and time travel.

www.tamaragill.com

Made in United States
Orlando, FL
18 May 2022

17996319R00098